TROUBLEMAKER

If anyone ha⸺ ⸺⸺ ⸺ that she'd stick arou⸺ ⸺ ⸺man instead of walki⸺ ⸺osh, she wouldn't ha⸺ ⸺eing so friendly. How⸺ ⸺e to spend some time with him?

Shyly, Julie looked up at Bruce. Now that they were alone, he seemed even more gentle. "Josh is a good guy," he said.

"Yes," Julie said in a soft voice.

"Is he your, you know . . ." Bruce let his question trail off.

"Boyfriend? No," Julie replied, realizing as soon as she said it that she'd jumped a little too fast to finish his sentence. "We're just good friends. Our parents are close, and we live next door to each other."

"Uh-huh," Bruce said, nodding. "That's good."

Julie swallowed and tried to compose herself to ask her next question. "Wh-what do you mean, Bruce?"

When Bruce turned to face her, his dark eyes seemed to burn right into hers. "I might as well ask you now. I've been meaning to ever since I saw you by your locker a couple of days ago."

Julie held her breath. Suddenly she felt a little light-headed.

"I know it's short notice," Bruce continued, "but would you like to go out on Friday night?"

Julie thought she must be dreaming. She didn't even have time to think before an ecstatic "Yes!" flew out of her mouth. She'd never been more sure about anything in her life—or more deliriously happy.

Bantam Books in the Sweet Valley High Series
Ask your bookseller for the books you have missed

SWEET VALLEY HIGH

TROUBLEMAKER

Written by
Kate William

Created by
FRANCINE PASCAL

BANTAM BOOKS
TORONTO · NEW YORK · LONDON · SYDNEY · AUCKLAND

RL 6, IL age 12 and up

TROUBLEMAKER
A Bantam Book / August 1988

Sweet Valley High is a trademark of Francine Pascal.

Conceived by Francine Pascal.

*Produced by Daniel Weiss Associates, Inc.
27 West 20th Street, New York, NY 10011*

Cover art by James Mathewuse.

ISBN 0-553-27359-0

Published simultaneously in the United States and Canada

*Bantam Books are published by Bantam Books, a division of Bantam Doubleday
Dell Publishing Group, Inc. Its trademark, consisting of the words "Bantam
Books" and the portrayal of a rooster, is Registered in U.S. Patent and
Trademark Office and in other countries. Marca Registrada. Bantam Books,
666 Fifth Avenue, New York, New York 10103.*

PRINTED IN THE UNITED STATES OF AMERICA

O   0 9 8 7 6 5 4 3 2 1

TROUBLEMAKER

One

"Arghhh!"

It never seemed to fail. Just when Elizabeth Wakefield got to the end of a beautiful melody on her recorder, she hit a clinker of a note.

Well, at least no one can hear me, she thought, looking around the soundproof practice room. For the last week she and Julie Porter had been playing duets in this room after school. At first Elizabeth had felt a little intimidated about learning the recorder from Julie. After all, Julie was one of the most talented musicians at Sweet Valley High. But Julie had turned out to be a wonderful teacher, patient and encouraging, and Elizabeth felt comfortable playing in front of her. This week Elizabeth was determined to

1

learn her parts perfectly, and it was worth giving up her lunch period on Monday to do it.

With a sigh she put the long wooden instrument to her lips again, took a deep breath, and blew.

As the door to the practice room flew open, the only sound that came out of the recorder was a loud, embarrassing squawk!

"Liz, you're just as bad as I was!" Jessica Wakefield remarked as she walked into the room.

"Well, if you hadn't barged in—"

Elizabeth turned to frown at her twin sister, ready to give her a lecture on respecting privacy. But when she saw how excited Jessica was, she just couldn't be annoyed anymore. Obviously there was something on her twin's mind that couldn't wait—something of absolute, earth-shaking importance, which, for Jessica, usually meant a new outfit or a cute guy who had started paying attention to her.

"Can we talk?" Jessica asked. She pulled up a chair, not waiting for an answer.

Elizabeth nodded. She knew she would hear every last detail no matter what she said. When her twin wanted to say something, she didn't let anything get in her way. It was just part of Jessica's personality. From a one-to-one conversation to the largest party, Jessica never failed to make herself the center of attention.

There was no one in the world whom Elizabeth felt closer to than Jessica. But even though they were twins, she couldn't imagine two people being more different—at least, in personality and interests—on the outside, Elizabeth knew that she and Jessica looked exactly alike. The hair that cascaded just past Jessica's shoulders was the same sun-streaked blond as Elizabeth's, her eyes the same sparkling blue-green. Every feature and every last detail matched, from their size-six figures to the dimples in their left cheeks. It was enough to keep classmates and teachers confused about who was whom.

"Liz, I have great news," Jessica blurted. "Guess who's going to be the biggest star in Sweet Valley High stage history!"

Elizabeth rolled her eyes. She hoped it wasn't another one of Jessica's crazy schemes to become a famous actress. How could she ever forget Jessica's debut in a drama club production—and the look of devastation on her face when DeeDee Gordon's movie-agent father had passed over Jessica and offered a screen test to her costar, Bill Chase?

"I thought *Splendor in the Grass* had gotten the theater bug out of your system," Elizabeth said.

Jessica shook her head. "That was just a warm-up. This really sounds like the role of a lifetime. It not only requires great acting, but dancing, too."

"Dancing? But you—"

"DeeDee Gordon told me all about it. She's the new president of the drama club. So I said that I knew ballet, and she mentioned it to Mr. Jaworski." Her face lit up. Mr. Jaworski was the drama coach. "And he personally asked me to come to the audition on Thursday! Isn't that great?"

Elizabeth laughed. "Jess, have you forgotten? You haven't taken ballet in years!"

"Oh, that won't really matter. I mean, we still have the barre set up in the basement, so I can practice from now till the audition. And besides, there's probably no one else trying out. DeeDee told me they wanted to cast it from the regular drama club members, but no one knew ballet. And there was no general audition notice. You know what that means. I have the inside track!"

The twins had both studied ballet when they were twelve years old. Elizabeth remembered the agony of doing endless pliés, relevés, and arabesques at Madame André's dance school. *Leave it to Jessica to think she can pick it all back up in four days*, Elizabeth thought. "I don't know about this, Jess. Are you sure you can do it?"

"Oh, Liz! Where's your sense of adventure? Really, sometimes I find it hard to believe that you and I are related."

4

Elizabeth smiled and nodded in agreement. For every ounce of enthusiasm Jessica had, Elizabeth had an equal ounce of common sense. Not only did it show in their personalities, but also in their style of dress. While Jessica wore trendy clothes, Elizabeth tended to be more casual and conservative. The two of them often joked that because Elizabeth had been born four minutes earlier than Jessica, she was more mature. Not that Elizabeth didn't have fun, but to her, fun didn't necessarily mean socializing and shopping. Elizabeth preferred to spend her free time reading, writing for *The Oracle*, Sweet Valley High's newspaper, or having long conversations with her best friend, Enid Rollins, or her steady boyfriend, Jeffrey French.

"Forget that I said that, Jess. Knowing you, I'm sure you can do it," Elizabeth said. "What play is it?"

"*You Can't Take It With You*. It's supposed to be a classic."

"You mean you haven't read it? How do you know what the part's like?"

Jessica laughed. "How could I have read it, Liz? I just heard about the audition today!"

Elizabeth nodded. "That's true. But aren't you going to go to the library and at least read the play?"

"Yeah, right, Liz. I'm going to spend time reading when my poor body has four years of catching up to do in ballet! This is going to take *all* my time and concentration, Liz. Practicing in every spare moment, strict dieting. . . ." With a sigh she rested her elbows on her knees and propped her chin up in her hands. "There's one problem, though."

"What's that?"

"Callbacks are the same night as the big Phi Epsilon party at Bruce Patman's house. Doesn't that figure? I mean, what am I going to do if I have to miss it?"

"Jess, I'm sure you'll have plenty of time to shower and change beforehand. The party's not till eight, and the audition is probably right after school. Besides . . ." Elizabeth paused. She knew she had to phrase her next words carefully. "I don't mean to be negative or anything, but don't you think you're jumping the gun a little bit? I mean, you don't know for sure that you'll even make the callback."

"Not make the callback?" Jessica's face showed wounded pride for a split second. Then she jumped up from the chair and put her feet in a perfect fifth position as she smiled at Elizabeth. "You must be kidding, Liz! Look at my form." She raised her chin in the air and leaned forward into an arabesque. It looked a little lopsided to Elizabeth, but she thought it best to keep her mouth shut. "Watch out, Baryshnikov, here I come!" Jessica proclaimed, sailing out of the practice room as quickly as she had come in.

Elizabeth turned back to her music. As she lifted her recorder to her lips, she couldn't help thinking that her sister was setting herself up for a big disappointment. Although with Jessica, you never knew. When she wanted something, she usually got it, whether it was a new outfit, a new boyfriend, or a part in the school play. Shaking her head, Elizabeth thought, *Wouldn't it be just like her to actually get the part?*

"I found this great new program," Johanna Porter said to her sister, Julie, as they walked down the hall. "Much better than the primitive one I showed you before. You can write music directly into the computer, and it's all driven by pull-down menus. You can even hook up a digital sampler and play right into the program— *and* you can correct your mistakes!"

"Whoa, wait a minute," Julie said with a laugh as she stopped in front of her locker. "I have no idea what you're talking about. What language are you speaking?" Johanna's transformation still amazed Julie. It wasn't long ago that her sister had been a high-school dropout, waitressing at a local restaurant. As the only one in the Porter family without musical ability, Johanna had felt incredibly inferior. But when she decided to give school another try, she discovered her hidden talents in science and technology. And now Julie was convinced that Johanna was turning into a computer engineer!

"Sorry," Johanna said, an embarrassed smile on her face. "I'll demonstrate it for you at home. I just know this will help your music writing."

Julie's face lit up with a fond smile as she looked into her sister's green eyes. She thought about how much their lives had changed since their mother's tragic death in an auto collision over six months before. When she was alive, the sound of Mrs. Porter's beautiful operatic voice had filled their house every day. After the accident, the house had seemed eerily quiet. But both girls had come a long way since then.

Julie was proud that her sister had pulled herself together and returned to school. Johanna had done it because she knew it had been her mother's deepest wish. But Julie often still felt stung by the tragedy. Her mother had always been the person she turned to whenever she was confused or depressed. Lately Julie had plunged into her music, practicing piano longer and harder than ever. It was so much easier to *play* what she was feeling rather than to open up to other people. All her life she had been labeled the shy, sensitive type. It wasn't that she didn't *like* other kids—she just didn't feel comfortable hanging out in big groups. There were always one or two close friends in her life, preferably ones who shared her love of music, such as Elizabeth Wakefield, her newest friend. Actually, Elizabeth and Julie had known each other for years. They had been very good friends back in Sweet Valley Middle School. But they had started hanging out with different crowds when they reached high school, and it was only in the last few weeks that they had grown close again. Julie was finally starting to feel she could really talk to Elizabeth about whatever was on her mind.

"Uh, sure, Johanna," Julie said. "I'd love to look at the program. Maybe after dinner. I'm going over to Elizabeth's to play duets in a few minutes."

"OK. I'll ask Dad if I can set it up for you on his computer. See you later!"

As Johanna disappeared down the hallway, Julie reached into her locker for her history book.

Suddenly she heard Elizabeth's voice behind her. "Don't try to hide from me, Julie. I mean, I know I make a lot of mistakes, but you agreed to practice with me today!"

"Oh, hi, Liz!" Julie answered. "Don't worry, I'm not hiding. Just give me a couple of minutes to get organized." The petite redhead stretched up on her toes to get a look at the top shelf. From a messy pile of loose-leaf papers, notebooks, and music manuscripts, she pulled out her book of recorder duets.

"Hey, I wonder what those guys are up to," Elizabeth said.

"What guys?" Julie asked.

"Bruce Patman, Ronnie Edwards, and Winston Egbert. They're standing around the corner in their Phi Epsilon jackets, staring at the lockers and laughing as if something really hysterical just happened."

Julie shrugged her shoulders. "Who knows?" She reached all the way to the back of the top shelf to grab her recorder case. "You know, they really don't make these lockers for short people. OK, I think I've finally got all my stuff. Ready?"

Elizabeth nodded. "I've already practiced a lot since last time."

"Great! I just found an incredibly gorgeous Renaissance piece that we could work on next. It's a lot harder, but—"

Suddenly Julie stopped talking. With a quizzical look she turned around toward the lockers.

"Did you forget something?" Elizabeth asked.

"No," Julie replied. She shrugged her shoulders. "I must be hearing things. I could have sworn I heard a noise coming from one of the lockers."

Elizabeth laughed. "Well, I'm sure you'll be hearing lots of strange noises, as soon as I start playing."

"Oh, come on, Elizabeth. You're starting to play really well. And I'm having a great time playing with you. You know, it's strange, but even though I come from a family of musicians, we all play alone. Dad's always in his study learning some new piece for the orchestra, and when Mom was alive she'd practice her singing all day, and I spend a lot of time on the piano. So I really look forward to our duets."

As they started down the hallway toward the front door of the school, a loud thumping noise made them stop in their tracks, and they both turned back to face the row of lockers.

"There it is again," Julie said. "And it *did* come from inside a locker!"

"Come on, let me out!" a muffled voice cried.

Julie and Elizabeth exchanged confused glances.

"What in the world . . ." Elizabeth muttered. Before she could say another word, the sound of laughter rang out from the other end of the hallway.

The two girls looked over and saw Bruce,

11

Winston, and Ronnie run around the corner in an attempt to hide.

"Haven't I been in here long enough, guys? Where are you?" the voice in the locker pleaded.

The laughing around the corner grew louder, and then someone said, "Go ahead, Egbert. You get him!"

Then, stumbling as if he had been pushed, Winston Egbert appeared in the hallway. Tall, gangly Winston was known as the junior class clown.

"Oh, uh, hi, Elizabeth. Hi, Julie. What's happening?" he asked, nervously running his fingers through his hair as he backed across the hallway toward the mysterious voice.

"I was just going to ask you that same question, Winston," Elizabeth replied.

"Oh! You must mean the, um, voice in there," he said, gesturing toward the locker.

"Mm-hmm," Elizabeth said, sounding suspicious. "You haven't become a ventriloquist, have you?"

Julie knew Winston liked practical jokes, but trapping someone in a locker was definitely too mean a trick for him to think of doing. "Winston, tell me that's a tape recording playing in there," she said.

"Uh, well, no," Winston answered, looking uncomfortable. "It's just a little joke, really. You see, it's pledging time for Phi Epsilon, and, well—"

A deep, assertive voice cut him off. "Terrific, Egbert! Talk to the girls while we're all waiting for you!"

They turned to see tall, athletic Bruce Patman striding toward them, glaring at Winston. Bruce belonged to one of Sweet Valley's wealthiest families, and it showed. He walked with a self-confident swagger, as if he owned the school. Aside from his fraternity jacket, everything he wore was the best, the most expensive, right down to his gold watch and his Italian glove-leather loafers. Right behind Bruce was Ronnie Edwards, doubled over with laughter. Ronnie was just as arrogant as Bruce. Elizabeth didn't like either of them.

Bruce shook his head as he passed Winston. "While you're running off at the mouth, the poor guy is going to die in there!"

Twirling the combination, Bruce yanked open the locker. A tall boy with brown hair peered out, his body scrunched up and drenched with sweat. His face turned beet red when he saw the two girls.

Julie's eyes widened with recognition. "Josh!" she exclaimed.

Josh Bowen flashed a sheepish smile as he squeezed out of the locker. "Hi, Julie."

"Cozy in there, huh, Bowen?" Bruce said to him with a smirk.

Josh smoothed down his shirt and stretched his arms over his head. "It really wasn't that bad."

"Well, I'm glad you feel that way," Bruce said smoothly, "because we have a whole list of activities planned for you out in back of school."

Josh gave a subdued nod. "Sure, Bruce," he mumbled.

"Hey," Bruce said with a cocky grin, putting his arm around Josh's shoulders, "is this the guy who was so crazy about joining the frat a couple of weeks ago? Look, Bowen, if you want to be in Phi Epsilon, this is the part that separates the men from the boys. We all went through it—me, Ronnie, your brother, even Winston. I don't know, though. Do you really think you've got what it takes?"

Josh looked right into Bruce's eyes with a defiant glare. The two of them were the same height and build, and for a minute Julie thought there was going to be a fight. But instead Josh inhaled deeply and said, "You better believe I do!" Pulling his shoulders back, he walked resolutely toward the back exit, followed by Ronnie.

Bruce glanced quickly at Elizabeth and Julie. Beneath his shock of dark brown hair his blue eyes glinted with mischief. After he checked out both girls, he smiled and gave them a quick wink before sauntering after Josh and Ronnie.

"I can't believe Josh let them do that!" Julie said, looking shocked. "Imagine being locked up like that. He must be so embarrassed."

"Yeah, he looked embarrassed. I don't really know Josh, I've never been in any classes with him. But I guess since he's your neighbor, you know him pretty well."

"That's right. We've been friends for years. He's one of the nicest people I know—really thoughtful, funny, and smart."

"He doesn't seem like the type of guy who would get mixed up with Bruce Patman and his crowd," Elizabeth observed.

"Well, he's dying to get into Phi Epsilon, and Bruce is a member. Josh's brother, Phil, was a member when he went to school here, and Josh absolutely worships him." Julie shook her head. "But when he told me he wanted to pledge, I didn't realize he'd have to do stuff like that!"

"That fraternity has really changed," Elizabeth said. "I mean, it used to be that pledging was fun, not mean."

"Really? How do you know that?"

"Well, my old boyfriend, Todd Wilkins, was a member." Elizabeth laughed and quickly added, "But believe me, he never went around torturing people. I think that must have started happening when Bruce became one of the ring-leaders. He certainly wasn't very nice to Josh just now!"

Julie shrugged her shoulders. "Well, I don't know. I feel sort of bad for Bruce—you know, because of Regina and all." Julie didn't really know Bruce, but she had seen him at school with Regina, and it was easy to tell they had been in love. And she knew he must have been devastated by Regina's sudden death, caused by a rare reaction to cocaine the one time she had tried it at a party. Julie looked at the ground. "I know what it's like when someone you love dies," she said softly.

Elizabeth nodded. "He seemed so happy when he was going with her. It was as if his whole personality changed." She sighed. "It's just so strange to see him acting like his old self again."

"Well, he must be under a lot of strain right now," Julie said. Then a smile inched across her face. "Besides, I think beneath the surface there's a sweet guy there. He's got such amazingly sensitive eyes."

Elizabeth raised an eyebrow. "Well, I *have* seen that side of him on occasion. But judging from the way he's been acting lately, I'm not so sure he's a sweet guy. You ought to ask my sister about the time she went out with him. I think *sensitive* is probably the last word she would have used to describe him. He really hurt her feelings."

"That's too bad. What did he do?"

As the two girls rode the bus home, Elizabeth described Jessica's unhappy fling with Bruce. But Julie found it hard to listen. Her thoughts kept wandering back to his beautiful blue eyes. She had seen Bruce around school, but he had never actually looked at her like that before.

Be realistic, Julie, she said to herself. *It's ridiculous to even think he'd consider going out with you.*

But there was something about that look. It had seemed much more meaningful than just a casual glance. Julie's heart raced. Maybe it wasn't so ridiculous after all.

Two

Elizabeth and Julie were both hunched over their music stands, and the sound of a Renaissance piece filled Elizabeth's bedroom. They kept going, ignoring a few small mistakes and building momentum as they neared the end of the piece. Elizabeth felt a sense of relief and triumph— the music sounded so wonderful!

Bleeeeeeeat!

Julie burst out laughing.

"Oops," Elizabeth said, looking sheepish. "I knew it was too good to be true!"

Just then there was a rapping at the door. "Hey, what's going on in there?" a muffled voice asked. "You've got all the dogs in the neighborhood howling!"

Elizabeth felt her face turn red as she opened the door. "Sorry, Mom. I thought you said you were going to be at a meeting. Really, I planned on sparing you the torture."

Alice Wakefield laughed as she set down her briefcase full of interior-design plans. With her youthful face and her blond hair cut in a page boy, she could have passed for Elizabeth's older sister. Her stylish paisley silk dress was just short enough to show her lean, athletic calves and was gathered at a waist that was every bit as slender as the twins'. "We finished early. The client agreed to everything right away. In fact, I'm still in shock." With a teasing look she continued, "But if I'd known I was coming home to this, I would have figured out a way to make the meeting last longer."

Julie and Elizabeth both giggled at Mrs. Wakefield's remark. "Well, actually," Elizabeth said, "we had planned on playing it through one more time before dinner."

"That's fine," Mrs. Wakefield said. "But I could use your help in the kitchen in a few minutes. You can call Jessica, too. She's in the basement."

"The basement? What's she doing down there?" Elizabeth asked.

"Practicing ballet, of all things." Mrs. Wakefield rolled her eyes. "After all that complaining a few years ago about how demanding ballet was, how tiring it was, and what an awful, old-fashioned teacher Madame André was. I'll never understand that girl."

"Oh, it's for an audition at school, Mom," Elizabeth said. "The drama club is doing a play, and Jess is trying out for a role that involves dancing."

"Mm-hmm," Mrs. Wakefield said, raising an eyebrow. She turned toward the door. "Just make sure our budding ballerina knows that she has to trade in her tutu for an apron before dinner."

As her mother walked out Elizabeth gave Julie an exasperated look. "I guess I need to work on this a lot more, huh?"

"Only a little, really. But let's give it a rest till next time," Julie answered. "That wasn't bad for a first reading, you know. Do you want to get together sometime on Friday?"

"Sure! Let's meet—" Elizabeth stopped to think about what she already had planned. "Wait a minute. Friday's a bad day for me. I have to work late at *The Oracle*, and then afterward Jeffrey and I are going to the Phi Epsilon party."

"That doesn't sound like such a bad day to me," Julie observed. "I'd be going, too, if it weren't for those stupid frat rules. Josh wanted to take me, but pledges aren't allowed to bring anyone to the party. Can you believe it?"

"I thought you told me you weren't going out with Josh," Elizabeth said.

"I'm not," Julie said, laughing. "I mean, Josh is a great guy and all, but well, you know, we've been such good friends for so long, it would be like going out with your brother or something." She picked up her recorder case and pulled out a cleaning brush. "It would have been fun to go to the party, though. My social life has been absolutely nonexistent lately."

Elizabeth nodded. It was too bad Julie felt that way about Josh, because he seemed like the perfect guy for her—someone who knew her well enough to help her through the pain she was feeling about her mother's death. Julie had once confided in Elizabeth about how sad she sometimes felt without her mother there to talk to, and Elizabeth had really grown to care about Julie. She wished there were something she could do to make Julie's life more cheerful.

"Look, Julie," Elizabeth said, "why don't you come with Jeffrey and me? It would probably be fun to just get out of the house for the evening, even if it's not a date. I'm sure you won't be the only one there who's not paired up with someone."

Julie smiled bashfully. "That's really sweet of you, Elizabeth. But—well, I wouldn't know what to do with myself whenever you guys went off dancing or something." She placed her recorder in its case. "I'd feel so self-conscious. Especially in front of some of those guys."

"Like who?" Elizabeth asked.

"Well, you know . . ."

Elizabeth remembered their earlier conversation. "You don't mean Bruce Patman, do you?"

"I guess . . ." Julie said, turning crimson.

"You really like him, don't you?"

"No, not exactly. I just think he's sort of nice looking." Julie picked up her case and shifted uncomfortably from foot to foot. "You know, those incredible blue eyes. . . . What can I say?" Julie's eyes lit up, and she lowered her voice as if someone might be listening to her deep, dark secret. "He's a hunk!" Julie let out a nervous giggle.

Elizabeth wanted to laugh with Julie, but she felt a little tense about the whole situation. Along with Julie's shyness, there was something very naive about her. That was one of her most refreshing and lovable qualities, but it made Elizabeth a little afraid for Julie. Julie was the last person she wanted to see hurt, especially by Bruce Patman, who seemed to be reverting to his old playboy behavior. So many girls had thrown themselves at Bruce's feet—some because of his sexy, handsome look, some because of his family's prestige in Sweet Valley, still others because they wanted to be seen riding with him in his black Porsche. And Bruce seemed willing and able to accommodate all of them, one after the other. When he got tired of one, usually after a week or so of dating, he just moved on to the next. After Jessica had been dumped by him, she remarked that the rest of the girls ought to take numbers, like a bakery or a delicatessen. Bruce's favorite word seemed to be "Next!"

"I don't know, Julie," Elizabeth said. She didn't want to butt in on Julie's personal life, but she felt a duty to warn her about Bruce. "Bruce has been through a lot lately. First of all, I don't think he's gotten over Regina. Second of all—well, I know you think he has a sensitive soul, and I don't want to tell you you're wrong or anything, but you've never seen his other, less considerate side. You should be careful around him, that's all."

Julie smiled at Elizabeth's solemn, earnest face. "Oh, I know. I guess I just have this thing about guys I know wouldn't even *dream* of looking at me. I always imagined some tall, dark, handsome type would hear me play outside my window and sweep me off my feet!" She laughed. "My mother always told me I was too much of a dreamer. I think she wanted me to go out with someone like Josh."

"Well, Josh is sort of a tall, dark, handsome type."

"*Sort of* is the important part of that description," Julie replied with a giggle. "I guess I'll just have to stick with my dreams. Anyway, Liz, I don't think you need to worry about me. A guy like Bruce Patman wouldn't notice me if I jumped up and bit him on the nose."

Elizabeth smiled. Looking at Julie's sweet face, her simple hairstyle, and her conservative clothes, she had to admit Julie was right. Bruce tended to go after much flashier types. "Well, it's none of my business anyway," she said.

"Oh, that's OK," Julie answered good-naturedly. Together the two girls walked down the stairs to the front door.

"Oh!" Julie exclaimed as she stepped outside. "We forgot to set up another time. How about Wednesday?"

"Wednesday's fine," Elizabeth said.

"And tell your mom we'll sound much better next time! Bye!"

As Elizabeth closed the front door behind Julie, she became aware of an odd but familiar set of noises—classical music combined with grunting and thumping sounds. Just then the music came to an abrupt stop, and an anguished cry rang out.

Elizabeth followed the cry to the basement door. She called down, "Jessica, are you OK?"

24

Jessica whirled around. Her hair was pulled back tightly into a neat ponytail. She wore a loose pink T-shirt with the sleeves and neck cut away and the faded words *American Ballet Theater* printed across the front. Her sweatpants were rolled up.

"Come down and close the door, quick!" Jessica said. "I don't want anyone to see me like this!"

"What are you talking about, Jess?" Elizabeth asked. Even in her strange dancer's getup, Jessica looked stylish. "You look terrific!"

"I can't believe you said that, Liz," Jessica answered without acknowledging the compliment. There was a look of frustration on her face. "I try to raise my leg to do an arabesque, and I feel like I need a forklift! I can't do a grand plié without feeling like I'm going to sink to the floor and never get up." She raised her hands and slapped them against her thighs in exasperation. "Liz, what am I going to do? I just can't make a total fool of myself in front of the drama club—they'll never let me be in anything again!"

"I'm sure it's not nearly as bad as you think." Elizabeth reassured her. "Don't expect the movements to feel natural right away. After all, your body's a little rusty. It hasn't done this in a long time."

"I know, I know," Jessica said. "You'd think I was thirty years old or something." She looked at Elizabeth with a sparkle of hope in her eyes. "Liz, you wouldn't mind watching me practice, would you? I mean, maybe you can see what I'm doing wrong and give me some pointers. Please? This is really important."

Elizabeth smiled at her sister's endless ambition. "Of course, Jess." She pulled up an old chair that she found in the corner of the basement and sat down. "We don't have much time before we have to help with dinner," she said, checking her watch. "Now, I'm not exactly sure how much I remember, but I'll try to help you."

Jessica flew into a series of pliés and relevés in each of the five positions. "Keep your back straight," Elizabeth suggested. "You're arching it, and it's throwing you off balance."

As Jessica danced Elizabeth gave her tips that strengthened and streamlined her movements. Within ten minutes Jessica was even able to manage a halfway decent pirouette.

"That was great!" Elizabeth said. "You looked like the star of Madame André's class all over again!"

Breathing heavily, Jessica grinned and grabbed a towel she had draped over the barre. "It is all coming back to me, you know." She sat down on the floor, stretched out her legs, and began massaging her left thigh. "So, how did your duets go with Julie this afternoon?"

Elizabeth could tell Jessica was feeling better—she was interested in something besides herself. "Well, playing was OK. But I'm a little worried about Julie."

"Why? What happened?"

"Nothing. It's what *might* happen. I think she's developing a serious crush on your favorite ex-boyfriend, Bruce Patman."

Jessica rolled her eyes. "Poor girl."

"I don't know what to do, Jess. She's so sensitive. I don't want to see her get hurt, the way you were."

Jessica stood up and stretched over, touching her toes easily. "I wouldn't worry about it too much, Liz. It's her business if she likes Bruce—even if it's crazy. And, no offense, but I kind of doubt Bruce would go after someone as quiet as Julie."

Elizabeth sighed. "I know. I'll try not to think about it." She checked her watch again. "OK, ready to do another couple of pirouettes before we call it quits?"

"I can do better than that!" Jessica said with renewed confidence. She began leaping around, a huge grin on her face. "This audition is going to be easy! I don't even know what I was worrying about!" Jessica exclaimed as she flew into a grand jeté.

"Yeow!" she cried, her face creased with pain as she landed soundly on the floor, her left leg underneath her. "Liz, help! I can't straighten my leg!"

Three

"It's the most incredible thing," Julie said to Elizabeth and Josh after taking a long sip of her milk shake. They were seated at a table in Casey's, the best place to go for ice cream in Sweet Valley. "Some of them actually grade papers, right there on stage during rehearsals. My dad told me."

Elizabeth couldn't believe her ears. She was listening so intently to Julie's story that the ice cream was melting in her Casey's Concoction, a special sundae covered with three different sauces and chocolate dust. "Are you kidding? Professional musicians do that during rehearsals? Doesn't the conductor notice?"

"Liz, this is the Los Angeles Symphony Orchestra. These are some of the top musicians in the area. As long as they play when they're supposed to, the conductor doesn't care. They know exactly when they have to start playing at all times."

"Beside, a lot of them are teachers," Josh added, chewing on the straw in his soda.

"Exactly," Julie continued. "So if they have a long enough rest, they can grade maybe one or two of their students' compositions!"

"Amazing," Elizabeth said. "I'd imagine that they'd be too swept up in the passion of the music. *I* would be."

"Not if you did it every day," Julie said. "I'm sure most of them started out with enough passion, but to them the symphony is their job, just like going to work for a law firm. Right, Josh? Isn't your mother that way?"

"Uh, yeah," Josh answered in a distracted tone, looking over his shoulder at something.

"Mrs. Bowen is the second chair clarinetist in the orchestra. She and my dad carpool sometimes." Julie smiled mischievously. "Josh, tell Elizabeth the story about what that bassoonist did with the trumpeter's mute. Josh?"

It seemed as if Josh hadn't even heard Julie. He was fiddling with his straw and looking around the room with a forced smile.

"Josh?" Julie repeated. "Are you all right?"

Josh turned back to the table with a start.

"Oh! Sorry, Julie. I was just daydreaming. Did you ask me something?"

"What's up, Josh?" Julie answered. "You're not acting like yourself today."

Josh puffed out his cheeks as he exhaled. "I don't know. I guess I'm a little nervous. A couple of the guys from Phi Epsilon are supposed to meet me here, and I have no idea what they're up to."

"Another pledge prank?" Elizabeth asked.

Josh shrugged his shoulders. "Could be. They didn't say." He drummed his fingers on the tabletop and mumbled, "I sure hope not. I don't know if I can deal with much more of this."

"If it's that bad, Josh," Julie said, "why don't you just quit?"

"Because most of the guys are really great. And everybody has to go through this period. There's a reason for it. Phil told me that once you get through the pledging and you get into the fraternity, you have an incredible feeling of accomplishment. And it automatically gives you something in common with your brothers that you'll share the rest of your lives."

"I can think of some other things you already have in commmon," Julie said. "Like eating, sleeping, breathing—things that you don't have to go through torture to experience."

Josh let out a tense laugh. "You know what I mean, Julie."

Just then the conversation was interrupted by the sound of loud, laughing voices just outside Casey's in the mall. Elizabeth, Julie, and Josh all turned around the door. Bruce Patman was the first of the Phi Epsilon brothers to barge in, followed by Ronnie Edwards, Michael Harris, Tom McKay, and Bill Chase. With a cocky smirk Bruce surveyed the restaurant.

Here we go, Elizabeth said to herself.

"Glad you could make it, Bowen!" Bruce said, strutting over toward their table. "Sorry we're late. I hope we didn't keep you waiting. Mind if we join you?"

"Where are your *manners,* Patman?" Ronnie Edwards said in mock dismay. "I'd say we should leave the guy alone. He's obviously enjoying himself without us."

"Of course, Ronald, right you are!" Smiling broadly, Bruce bowed to the table. "Pardon me, Josh, ladies." With that, he walked over to the counter with the other four fraternity brothers following close behind.

"Well, that wasn't *too* painful," Julie commented.

"I don't think they're done yet, Julie," Josh said worriedly.

Sure enough, the five boys eventually settled in at the table next to theirs. Each of them carried two enormous ice-cream dishes—Casey Concoctions, sundaes, and banana splits, all dripping with whipped cream and toppings of marsh-mallow, hot fudge, chopped nuts, and fruit.

"Are they really going to eat all that?" Julie whispered.

She and Elizabeth looked at Josh for an answer, but all he could muster was a nervous gulp as he grew more and more flustered.

"Look, we're all finished—maybe we should go," Elizabeth suggested.

But Josh ignored her, a look of gloom on his face as he clenched and unclenched his hands.

At the other table Bruce and his friends each devoured one of their sundaes in two or three minutes. Then they pushed aside their empty dishes, still leaving five huge desserts untouched.

"Hits the spot, doesn't it?" Tom McKay said in a loud voice. He pushed his chair back from the table and patted his stomach. "I could eat three of these!"

"Mustn't be selfish, Thomas," Bruce said. "I mean, look at the table next to us. A future brother of ours sits starving while we feast like kings. I ask you, is that fair? Is that the way we treat our brothers in Phi Ep?"

"No!" the four others called out.

"Well, then, I think we ought to summon up all our brotherly generosity and sacrifice our seconds to a worthy cause—the care and feeding of a Phi Epsilon pledge!"

Immediately all five boys stood up and placed

the remaining desserts in front of Josh, who looked as if he were about to be given a flu shot. Glancing up at Bruce, Josh smiled weakly. "You don't expect me to eat *all* of these, do you?" he asked, a note of hope in his voice.

"Of course not!" Bruce said and then shrugged. "Unless, of course, you want to be in Phi Epsilon."

The five brothers stared at Josh with amused anticipation on their faces. Elizabeth and Julie stared at Josh, too, anxious to see what he would do. Josh glanced from face to face. Elizabeth could see little beads of sweat forming on his forehead. She hoped he'd had enough and that he would tell Bruce off and leave.

But instead, looking like a person who had resigned himself to a life sentence in jail, Josh picked up a spoon and dug into the banana split.

With a mixture of anger and disgust, Elizabeth watched as Josh ate the entire split and went on to one of the sundaes.

"Good stuff, huh?" Bill said.

"Only the best for our pledges," Ronnie chimed in. "And don't forget, it's on us."

Josh managed a half-smile and dug to the bottom of the sundae. He pushed it aside with a quarter inch of thick hot-fudge sauce still on the bottom.

"I don't know, Bowen, it looks like you left the best part in the dish. You know how great

Casey's hot fudge is. I'm sure you want to eat every last bite," Bruce scolded, pushing the sundae back in front of Josh.

Josh polished off the hot fudge, and after that he ate the Casey's Concoction, not slowing down a bit. The next dessert was a huge glass filled with pistachio ice cream that had been mixed with several kinds of candy and nuts. Four chocolate-chip cookies stuck out of the sides, and topping the whole thing were crushed pineapple, butter-scotch sauce, and an inch or two of whipped cream. Casey called this one his Diet Breaker.

Elizabeth felt sick just seeing Josh look at it. She wanted to say something, but she knew it would be useless. Slowly Josh poked his spoon into the ice cream. He seemed to be using all his concentration, taking it one bite at a time, as if each bite might land in a corner of his stomach that still happened to be empty.

Suddenly, without warning, Josh dropped the spoon. His face became pale as he pushed himself away from the table. For a minute Elizabeth thought he was going to faint. But instead he grabbed his stomach with one hand and his mouth with the other, jumped up from his chair, and ran out the front door.

Josh's cheeks finally began to regain their color as Julie walked him slowly around the mall parking lot. "That's it, take deep breaths," she said, pausing every few steps with him.

"Thanks, Julie," Josh said between gasps. "I really thought I could do it without getting sick."

"Don't be silly, Josh. That was more than any normal human could possibly eat. You'll probably be in sugar-shock for days."

Julie wanted to be cheerful for Josh and pretend that the whole incident had been funny, but inwardly she was extremely angry at Bruce and the rest of the Phi Epsilon members. Bruce might be gorgeous to look at, but his behavior had really shattered Julie's impression of him. She led Josh to the curb where Elizabeth was sitting, and they both sat down.

"Feeling better?" Elizabeth asked.

"Yeah, thanks," Josh said. "Listen, I'm all right now. Really, don't stick around here just because of me."

Julie felt a rush of warmth for her old friend. In all the years she had known Josh, he had been so easygoing and on top of things compared to her. He was always the one calming her down. Nothing ever seemed to faze him. It was strange to see him so upset like this, so vulnerable. Julie felt as if she were seeing Josh for the first time, as a sensitive boy who wanted other people's approval. Actually, she always knew how much the approval of his older brother, Phil, meant to him, but Josh didn't usually care so much about the opinion of guys like Bruce Patman. Julie suspected Phil was the main reason Josh was interested in the fraternity in the first place.

Phil Bowen had graduated from Sweet Valley High two years earlier. He had been immensely well liked and involved in lots of school activities. Now a sophomore at Princeton, he had been class valedictorian as well as the president of his senior class. Julie knew that Josh respected his brother a great deal and wanted to follow in his footsteps. Obviously, he thought he could start by becoming a member of the same fraternity Phil had joined when he was in high school. Julie hated seeing Josh look so defeated. She felt like hugging him, telling him she was his friend and that everything would be all right. But just imagining doing that made Julie feel embarrassed. It would be so out of character, he'd think she was being totally weird. Instead, she squeezed his hand and said, "Just relax, Josh. We're not in any hurry." She smiled. "Besides, you still haven't told Elizabeth the story of the bassoonist—"

Julie was cut off by a voice behind her. "Excuse me, girls. Is he OK?"

Oh, no. Bruce doesn't feel he's tortured Josh enough, Julie thought. *He's got to come rub it in.* She felt a scream building inside her. She whirled around, ready to tell Bruce off, ready to say that of all the worthless creeps in Phi Epsilon, he was the worst.

But when Julie saw the look of deep concern on his face, all her angry feelings melted away. Bruce's expression was apologetic. In his hand was a glass of club soda with ice.

"I guess we got a little carried away in there," he said. "It's all my fault. I don't know, it seemed pretty harmless when I thought only one or two guys were going to come with me. I didn't expect so many of the guys to tag along. You two must think we're a bunch of barbarians."

"That might be too complimentary. But maybe you should apologize to Josh, not us," Elizabeth suggested.

"Of course," Bruce said. He sat down next to Josh and put his arm around Josh's shoulder. "Sorry, buddy. I guess my big-shot instincts got the best of me. It won't happen again. Here, drink this club soda. It'll settle your stomach."

Josh managed a small smile. "Thanks, Bruce. Don't worry about it. I guess I'll be guilty of the same mistakes when I'm initiating pledges."

Bruce is really a nice guy, Julie thought. *Not only to admit his mistake, but to apologize to Josh in front of Liz and me*. She smiled at Josh and said, "Well, look at it this way. Bruce has probably cured you of a sweet tooth."

Bruce laughed. "Hey, she's right. I've probably done you a favor, considering each trip to

Casey's is roughly equal to one and a half cavities."

"I know what you mean," Julie said. "Every time I go to the dentist I vow never to come here again." She shrugged her shoulders. "It never works."

Bruce gave Julie a sexy, lopsided smile. "I'm glad. The only reason I come here is because it's where all the prettiest girls hang out."

Julie felt her face getting warm. Out of the corner of her eye she caught a glimpse of Elizabeth, who looked a little skeptical. "Julie," Elizabeth said, "I've really got to get home. Want to go?"

If anyone had told Julie five minutes ago that she would stick around with Bruce Patman instead of driving home with Elizabeth, she wouldn't have believed it. But Bruce was being so friendly. How could she pass up this chance to spend some time with him? "Why don't you go on ahead, Elizabeth. I don't want to keep you. I, uh, left some of my music inside, and I can always get the bus."

Elizabeth looked surprised by Julie's answer. "Oh, well, maybe I can stick around," she said. "The buses don't come very often."

"No," Julie insisted. "You go ahead. I—I want to pick up some sheet music at the music store."

"I'll ride with you," Josh said to Elizabeth, slowly standing up. "I've got to get back, too.

My car's in the garage, and I can't pick it up till tomorrow."

Elizabeth gave Julie a glance as if to say, "Will you be all right?"

Julie understood the look, and she smiled at Elizabeth to assure her that she felt perfectly fine. "See you guys tomorrow!" she said cheerfully and waved to them as they started toward the Fiat Spider Elizabeth and Jessica shared.

Shyly Julie looked up at Bruce. Now that they were alone, he seemed even more gentle. "Josh is a good guy," he said.

"Yes," Julie said in a soft voice. *Why do I feel as though I don't have a thing to say?* she thought. *How are we ever going to have a conversation?*

"Is he your, you know . . ." Bruce let his question trail off.

"Boyfriend? No," Julie replied, realizing as soon as she said it that she had jumped a little too fast to finish his sentence. "We're just good friends. Our parents are close, and we live next door to each other."

"Uh-huh," Bruce said, nodding. "That's good." He looked off into the distance.

Julie swallowed and tried to compose herself to ask her next question. "What do you mean, Bruce?"

When Bruce turned to face her, his eyes seemed to burn right through hers. "I might as well ask you now. I've been meaning to since I saw you by your locker a couple of days ago."

Julie held her breath. Suddenly she felt a little light-headed.

"I know it's short notice," Bruce continued, "but are you free Friday night?"

Julie thought she must have dreamed Bruce's question. Friday was the night of the party. Was he going to ask her to go with him? *Easy, Julie, he must want you to help with the party's catering or something,* she told herself. Still, her mouth was too dry to manage anything but a stifled-sounding "Yes, I am."

"Great!" Bruce's face broke into the most attractive smile Julie had ever seen. "Then how would you like to go to the Phi Ep party with me?"

Julie didn't even have time to think before an ecstatic "Yes!" flew out of her mouth. She had never been more sure of anything in her life—or more deliriously happy.

Four

"How's this?" Jessica held up a shocking blue French-cut leotard for her best friend, Lila Fowler, to see.

"It's a very good color for you," the saleswoman said.

Lila raised an eyebrow as she examined it. "It *is* sexy. Try it on."

Jessica stepped into the dressing room. On a bench against the wall was a huge pile of leotards she had already tried on and decided against. Slipping this one on, she admired herself in the mirror. *I may not be a flawless ballerina*, she thought, *but there are some other things that should count at an audition*. She massaged her left hamstring gently, happy that she had suffered only a minor strain the day before.

The saleswoman was looking at her watch when Jessica emerged. "What do you think?" Jessica asked, turning around.

"Looks fabulous with your eyes, but the pink one shows off your body more," Lila said.

Jessica stood in front of a three-way mirror. She had to admit that Lila was right, as usual. Lila's shopping sense was the best of anyone Jessica knew, probably due to the countless hours Lila spent buying things for herself. Fashion was the one subject in which Lila never failed to do her homework. The Fowlers were one of the richest families in Sweet Valley, and Lila never ran out of ways to get her father to part with some, if not all, of his money.

"You're right," Jessica agreed, scrutinzing herself one more time in the mirror. "I'll take it." She sifted through the stack of leotards and handed the pink one to the saleswoman. She closed the door to the dressing room and quickly changed back into her miniskirt and cropped cotton sweater.

"I think you made the right decision," Lila said as Jessica opened the door and stepped out. "You'll either walk away with that part, or they'll lock you up for indecent exposure."

"Oh, stop, Lila," Jessica said, giggling. "It's the exact same style *everybody's* wearing." At that moment a tall blond girl came out of one of the dressing rooms, wearing a similar leotard in

43

white, with cream-colored tights and ankle warmers. "See, look at her."

As the girl walked toward a full-length mirror along the wall, Jessica and Lila both followed her with their eyes. She didn't seem to be walking as much as gliding. Her head was held high, and her back was arched gracefully. Instead of pointing forward, her feet were turned out to the sides.

"Yeah, look at her," Lila muttered. "She's got that ballerina walk down pat. Duck feet and all."

"She looks familiar," Jessica said.

Lila nodded. "Danielle Alexander," she said. "She's a senior." She sneered slightly and whispered, "She thinks she's really great. *I* think she's got an attitude problem."

Danielle adjusted the top of the leotard. Then, in a flurry of motion, she whirled into a dazzling series of fouetté turns, each one as amazingly perfect as the last.

Jessica felt her mouth fall open in awe. "Lila, she's incredible."

"So what? Obviously she takes ballet lessons. Big deal."

"Well, what's she doing here? Why is she buying a leotard *today?*"

They watched as Danielle continued to stare at her outfit in the mirror, occasionally doing graceful little pliés and then flexing and pointing her toes.

"Oh, I get it," Lila said with a knowing nod. "You're worried she's going to show up at the audition and steal your part, aren't you?"

"Well, wouldn't *you* be?" Jessica retorted. "I mean, I don't stand a chance against someone like that!"

Lila laughed. "You're so paranoid! Look, a person that good is probably a real ballerina."

"No kidding, Lila. Is that supposed to make me feel better?"

"Jessica, to get to be that good, what do you think a person has to do?"

"Practice like crazy! What else?"

"Exactly! Lessons every day, right? Six, seven days a week?"

"Probably."

"Then come the competitions, right? And then a spot in a ballet corps or something."

The conversation was beginning to frustrate Jessica. She was feeling more and more nervous about her competition, and all Lila was doing was pointing out how much better the other girl was. "Look, I don't have all day, Lila. What's your point?"

"The point is, she's too good to try out for a drama club play. Besides, even if she wanted to, she'd probably be too busy! She wouldn't have time for the audition, never mind rehearsals."

Jessica realized that Lila was probably right.

A school production of *You Can't Take It With You* wouldn't be worth the time of a professional-caliber dancer like Danielle. But if there were only some way to know for sure. . . .

"Miss, are you paying with cash or a credit card?" the saleswoman called from behind the register at the counter.

"Oh! Well, let me see," Jessica said, frantically thinking up a way to meet Danielle. She walked over to the counter and looked at the price tag again. "Hmm. I'd like to pay cash, but this is a little expensive, with tax and all. I'm wondering if there's another outfit, similar but maybe a little less expensive, like—" She turned and glanced around the room until her eyes rested on Danielle. In a louder voice she continued. "Like that outfit over there. Now, how much is that?"

The saleswoman rolled her eyes. "Look, I have other customers. When you're ready to buy something for sure, let me know, OK?"

As Jessica had hoped, Danielle heard her comment. The girl looked at Jessica and gave a halfhearted, slightly aloof smile. "It's pretty expensive," she said, holding out the price tag for Jessica to see. "It's this company's top of the line."

Jessica walked over and pretended to consider the price. "I see what you mean. Well, I just need something for this one *audition*. I wouldn't want to spend a fortune in case the *audition* didn't work out."

Danielle's face brightened. "Oh, are you trying out for the Los Angeles Ballet Company, too?"

"The Los Angeles Ballet Company?" Jessica repeated. "Uh, no. Are they holding auditions this week?"

"Next week," Danielle answered.

"No kidding. Well, good luck. I hope you get in."

"Thanks." Danielle turned in front of the mirror again. "By the way, do you like this?"

"It looks fantastic," Jessica said with a broad smile. "I'm sure it'll be worth every penny."

When Jessica went back to the counter, Lila was waiting for her, a sly gleam in her eyes. "Good work, Jess," she said. "I couldn't have done better myself."

"I'll take that pink one after all," Jessica said to the saleswoman. "Cash."

"I was right, wasn't I?" Lila asked.

"Lila, you're a genius. As far as I can see now, there's only one thing I need to worry about."

"What's that?"

Jessica grinned. "That the auditorium doesn't collapse during the deafening roar of applause at my curtain call!"

It wasn't until after lunch at school the next day that Julie finally saw Josh.

47

"Hey, stranger!" she called out as he came down the stairs from the second floor. "Where have you been?"

"Well," Josh answered, "I didn't have much of an appetite today, so I spent lunch period in the library."

Julie grabbed his arm compulsively. "Walk with me to social studies," she said. "I have to tell you something."

"What's gotten into you?" Josh said, laughing as Julie dragged him to a more secluded area of the hallway. "Did you win some sort of piano competition or something?"

Julie could hardly contain herself. "No, nothing like that. I'm going to your frat party Friday night."

"Well, great! I knew you'd come around. I'm sure you'll meet some nice people there—"

"No, Josh. You don't understand. I have a date!"

"Oh, really? Anyone I know?"

"Bruce Patman!"

Josh looked as though someone had just thrown ice-cold water in his face. "What? You're joking, right?"

"I know, I know. I couldn't believe it when he asked me, either. But it's true! He says he wants to get to know me better, and the party would be the perfect opportunity. I think he likes me!"

"And you said yes? Just like that?"

Julie was disappointed by Josh's reaction. She had expected him to be happy. "Well, yes. Did I do something wrong? I mean, I know he was a little mean and arrogant yesterday, but he went out of his way to apologize, and he was so sweet—"

"Sweet? Julie, I know it's none of my business, but, well, to tell you the truth, I don't think Bruce is worth the time of day from you. He's more than just arrogant, he has a really bad reputation, Julie!"

"Well, he's *your* future fraternity brother, Josh. If he's so awful, why are you even bothering to pledge Phi Epsilon? You must see something worthwhile in all those guys if you're dying to be one of them!"

"That's different, Julie. I mean, being a brother is one thing. I can put up with Bruce if there's a bunch of other guys around. But as a boyfriend? He's just not that nice to—"

"What's the big deal, Josh? I mean, I'm not saying I'm going to *marry* the guy! Besides, who are you to tell me what I should or shouldn't do with my personal life?"

"I'm sorry, Julie," Josh said quietly. "All I meant to say was that you should be careful. I wouldn't want to see you get hurt."

"Thank you for having so much confidence in my ability to judge people," she said bitterly, feeling confused and hurt. Part of her wanted to scream at Josh, but another part of her thought that he might be right.

She looked into Josh's face and saw his deep brown eyes staring back at her with concern. A nagging, hopeful thought came to her mind. Josh could be wrong. Maybe Bruce really *did* like her. Maybe Josh was only badmouthing Bruce because he was jealous—after all, he had wanted to take her to the party first.

Josh reached out to put a hand around Julie's shoulder, but before he had a chance, Julie spun around and raced down the hallway. She wasn't going to let him spoil her day any further.

Five

"Rejected again," groaned Jeffrey French, grasping his sandy blond hair in exaggerated frustration. "I don't know how much longer my fragile ego can take this!"

Elizabeth giggled. She could understand why her boyfriend was teasing her. After all, she had turned down an offer to go to the Dairi Burger with him on Monday, and today she had told him she couldn't ride home with him—both times because of practice sessions with Julie.

"Well, why do you always wait until after last period to ask me?" she asked in an accusatory tone.

"If I'd asked you earlier, would you have said yes?"

"Well, no . . ." Elizabeth answered. She looked playfully into his green eyes. "But at least you'd have the satisfaction of making me feel guilty the rest of the day."

With a laugh Jeffrey threw his arm around her. Elizabeth dissolved into giggles and made a weak effort to break away. But in truth she was completely happy in Jeffrey's arms, and she wouldn't want to be anywhere else. They had been a steady couple for several months now, and their feelings for each other seemed to get stronger by the day.

"Hey, let go of that woman before I report you for assault with intent to kiss!" a familiar voice threatened from down the hall.

Elizabeth looked up. "Enid!" she called out, spotting her best friend walking toward them. "Just in time to save me from the Sweet Valley Maniac!"

Jeffrey let go of Elizabeth as Enid pretended to scold him. "This is a high school, not a professional wrestling arena, you know. And this girl needs to be in one piece for a big party Friday night, so leave her alone." Her face broke into a grin as she tossed back her curly brown hair. "Which reminds me, can you give me a ride to the party? Hugh has to go to a basketball game at his school, so it'll just be me."

"Well, who knows, Enid? I may be going to the party by myself, too. That is, if Elizabeth decides she wants to practice the recorder that night."

"What?" Elizabeth said.

"I know what you mean, Jeffrey," Enid said. "These days, whenever I call her up at home, she's either practicing or listening to classical music." She sighed. "I guess you and I have been displaced in Elizabeth's life by an old wooden stick—or is it plastic?—with holes."

"Hey, come on, you guys!" Elizabeth protested. "It takes time to learn a new instrument. Besides, today's the last day we're practicing this week. So you can definitely save my seat in the car Friday."

"OK. I just hope you remember how to dance to modern music," Enid said slyly. "I don't think they'll be playing too many Renaissance songs."

"I think I'll manage," Elizabeth said dryly. After giving Jeffrey a quick kiss goodbye, she hurried off in the direction of the orchestra room. As she approached it she heard a gorgeous classical recording, a piano piece, incredibly rich and passionate. From her recent exposure to classical music, she tried to figure out what the piece was. Probably Chopin, she thought, played by one of the greats—Horowitz or Rubinstein. . . . But as she got closer she realized it wasn't a recording at all. Someone was actually in there, playing.

All at once it dawned on her who it was. Julie had said she would be practicing the piano that afternoon before their session. Sure enough, Elizabeth walked into the room and saw Julie playing on a mahogany baby grand. Her playing was so beautiful, Elizabeth didn't have the heart to interrupt. She sat down behind Julie to listen quietly.

Julie's fingers were flying over the keyboard so fast, Elizabeth could barely see them. The lyrical, romantic section had given way to an unbelievably fast passage. As far as Elizabeth could tell, Julie made absolutely no mistakes. And as the romantic section refrained at the end, Julie's playing seemed to make the piano cry with emotion. She finished the piece with a grand flourish.

The final chord echoed magnificently through the room. Unable to help herself, Elizabeth burst into applause.

Julie gasped and turned around with a start. "Oh, Liz! I didn't hear you come in!"

"Sorry, Julie," Elizabeth said. "I didn't mean to scare you. That was beautiful. I've never heard you seriously play the piano before. You play with such incredible feeling!"

Julie smiled. "Thanks. I wish I could play like

that all the time. But my playing always seems to match my mood."

"Well, judging from the way you were playing, you must be on cloud nine today!"

"Yeah, I guess you're right," Julie said, blushing.

"What's going on? Did something happen?" Elizabeth asked.

"Uh-huh. I know you're not going to believe this, but Bruce Patman asked me to the Phi Epsilon party Friday night!"

"Bruce *Patman?*" Elizabeth asked.

"Yes, isn't that amazing? It happened yesterday at the mall, right after you left."

Elizabeth tried not to show how shocked she was. She didn't want to upset her friend. "Wow. That's great." She wanted to be happy for Julie, but she couldn't help being suspicious. Bruce had to be up to something. He barely even knew Julie. Trying to look nonchalant, she said, "So, do you have your recorder here?"

Julie's ecstatic expression suddenly faded. "You look like I just told you about a train crash or something! What's wrong? Don't you approve?"

Elizabeth shrugged her shoulders. "Well, it's not up to me to approve or disapprove, Julie. I'm glad you have a date for the party."

"But you're not so glad about who the date *is*, right?"

"Well . . ."

Julie gave a half-smile. "That's OK, Elizabeth. You're not the first one to recognize that I'm falling under the dreadful influence of the ogre of Sweet Valley High!" She let out a small laugh. "Don't worry. I can take care of myself."

Try as she could, Elizabeth was unable to imagine why Bruce would ask Julie to the party. If he wanted to make his ex-girlfriend, Amy Sutton, jealous, he would have asked someone truly stunning. *Something strange is going on*, Elizabeth thought.

"Anyway, to answer your question, of course I brought my recorder," Julie continued, walking over to a corner of the music room. "Don't I always?" She grinned. "Shall we get started?"

"Sure," Elizabeth said, and she leaned down to pick up her instrument. But she couldn't get Bruce and Julie's date off her mind. *Julie really doesn't know what she's getting into with him*, Elizabeth thought. *She doesn't understand how devious he can be. And I wouldn't be a good friend if I didn't warn her.* As the two of them walked into a smaller practice room, Elizabeth said, "Before we start, I need to talk to you about something."

Julie had already sat down and begun to assemble her recorder. "Sure," she said. "What is it?"

"It's about this thing with Bruce, Julie. I know how excited you are. Bruce *is* a very gorgeous and popular guy. And sometimes he's really considerate and polite, too. But I just thought, as a friend, I should warn you not to get your hopes up too high. He's not always the most honest guy in the world and—"

"And he's going to use me and then spit me out when he gets tired of me, right? He's going to humiliate me and break my heart the way he's broken scores of other hearts before mine." Julie frowned and exercised her fingers on the recorder. "You know, I'm not as naive as I look. Everyone thinks I'm so *helpless*. Well, it's not true. I'm a fairly good judge of character, and I'm also pretty smart. I can figure out why Bruce has such a bad reputation. I'm sure that half the girls who fall for him are only after his money. No wonder he dumps them so quickly! And if you're afraid that he's only interested in seeing me for this one date, at least I'll have a fun time at the party! I mean, *you* were the one who told me I spent too much time at home practicing."

Elizabeth felt embarrassed. She *had* said that to Julie. Maybe going to the party was the best thing for her. At least now she would have a chance to meet a new crowd of people. And even though Julie was blind when it came to Bruce's faults, she sounded as if she had thought the whole thing through. "You're right, Julie," she said. "I'm sorry for sounding so negative. I *am* really happy for you."

Julie's face softened, and she turned to Elizabeth with a smile. "Oh, that's OK, Liz. It's just funny how when things start to go my way for the first time, nobody seems to be on my side."

"Well, *I'm* on your side. In fact, you've even got me sharing your taste in music. Which reminds me," Elizabeth said, taking the Renaissance piece out of the music folder in her book bag. "Why don't we give this a shot again? I think I know it."

"Good idea. I just hope I can keep up with you! Let's take it from the top, way under tempo. . . ."

"Jessica! Dinner!" Mrs. Wakefield called out.

Elizabeth finished setting the table as her father placed a steaming plate of veal cutlets on the table. Mrs. Wakefield brought in a large salad and a bowl of mashed potatoes, and the three of them sat down to eat.

"I hope she heard me through all that ballet music," Mrs. Wakefield said.

"I'll get her, Mom," Elizabeth replied, pushing her chair back from the table. At that moment in walked Jessica—but not the Jessica they knew. She swept through the entryway between the kitchen and dining room as if she were making an entrance onto a stage. Her head was held unusually high, and her hair was pulled back tightly in a ballerina's bun. As she walked to the dinner table, she pointed her feet ever so slightly outward.

"Uh, excuse me, but would you mind asking my daughter Jessica to join the four of us for dinner?" Mrs. Wakefield asked politely.

"Very funny, Mom," Jessica said. "Did you bring out those carrot sticks I cut up this afternoon?"

"They're right next to the veal cutlets," Mr. Wakefield said. "I guess we forgot about the hors d'oeuvres. But there's some onion dip in the fridge."

"That's all right, Dad," Jessica said. "That dip has dairy products in it. Very high fat content. Besides, these aren't hors d'oeuvres anyway. They're my main course—I mean, my *entree*." She reached out her left hand, grabbed a carrot stick, and took a bite. She chewed it slowly, a bored expression on her face.

"No!" Mr. Wakefield said in make-believe shock. "Is this the same Jessica Wakefield I've come to know and love? The one who could always be counted on to eat an entire batch of popcorn right after a full dinner and dessert? Or is this merely an impostor?"

"Boy, you're a supportive family, aren't you?" Jessica said, taking a bite of another carrot stick.

"My audition just happens to be tomorrow, you know. I shouldn't be eating *this* much—ballet dancers have to be *thin!*"

"I see," Mrs. Wakefield said seriously. "Well, I guess I'll just have to settle for some of those absolutely exquisite-looking veal cutlets, Ned. And you can put an extra dollop of your famous gravy on top of my mashed potatoes, please."

"OK, sweetheart," Mr. Wakefield said, taking her bait. "And how about some salad? Would you like a few extra slices of fresh, juicy garden tomatoes?"

Elizabeth watched Jessica as her face clouded over. Jessica's eyes followed the veal cutlets as they were passed across the table. Quickly she grabbed another carrot stick and ate it. Her face seemed to take on a sadness, as if she were making the world's grandest sacrifice. Elizabeth couldn't stand it anymore. She had to change the subject, or she knew she would burst out laughing and make her sister even angrier.

"Well, Jeffrey bought me some new cologne yesterday," she said. "A lady in a department store sprayed him by mistake, and he liked it! So he bought some for me. I think I'll wear it to the party Friday night."

"Sounds like this party is a pretty big deal," Mrs. Wakefield observed.

"I don't know," Elizabeth answered. "To tell you the truth, I can't get that excited about it."

"Why not?" her mother asked.

"Well, I've never been a big fan of fraternity parties. And I'm a little worried about this one. Julie's all excited because Bruce Patman asked her to be his date. But that just doesn't sound like him. I think something strange might be going on, like maybe some pledge trick."

"You never know, Liz," Alice Wakefield said. "Bruce has been through a lot of changes lately. Maybe he's really interested in Julie."

Jessica's face was crunched up in a puzzled expression. "Well, I know Bruce is interested in someone new, but I also know it isn't Julie. In fact, I heard he asked another girl to the party. Maybe his first choice turned him down."

Elizabeth felt a knot in her stomach. "What? Who, Jessica?"

Jessica shrugged her shoulders and picked a couple of bread crumbs off a veal cutlet. "Oh, I don't know who it is. It's only a rumor, anyway."

"Well, who told you?"

"Lila. One of the guys in Phi Ep told her."

"That's terrible. Julie's all set to go with Bruce. She thinks he's really sincere."

"That's all I know, Liz. I really don't think you should worry about it, though. Like I said, it's only a rumor." Jessica stood up from the table. Her expression had gone from self-pity to triumph. "I know it's early, but please excuse me. I've got to get back to practicing before my leg muscles stiffen up. See you later!"

Before she turned to leave, Jessica grabbed the smallest piece of veal and popped it in her mouth. Then she bounded out of the dining room, leaving Elizabeth deep in thought.

She had no idea if anything was going on with Bruce and someone else, but if there was anything worth getting excited about, Lila Fowler was sure to know about it.

Six

When Elizabeth approached Lila during lunch on Thursday, it was the third time she had tried to talk to her. Lila always seemed to be *with* someone, gossiping, laughing, flirting. But now she was sitting alone at a table in the cafeteria, busily scribbling a note on a sheet of gold-leaf stationery that had her initials printed at the top.

"Hi, Lila," Elizabeth said, putting her lunch tray down on the table. "Anyone sitting here?"

Lila looked up. "Oh, hi." She gestured to the seat across from her. "You can sit down. I have something I want to talk to you about."

Elizabeth was surprised. Usually the only time Lila wanted to talk to her was when she mistook her for Jessica. "Good, I have something I want to ask you, too. You go first."

"All right." Lila leaned close, then looked both ways to make sure no one was listening. "I'm having this problem. I've gone out with John Pfeifer a couple of times recently—you know, a movie here, a party there, nothing serious. Now all of a sudden he's calling me every day, sometimes *twice* a day. I think he's really gotten hung upon me."

"Well, what's wrong with that? John's a nice guy. Don't you like him?" John, a friend of Bruce Patman's, was the sports editor of *The Oracle*, so Elizabeth knew him fairly well. But it was unusual for Lila to be discussing her love life with *her*, Elizabeth thought. Maybe Lila *did* think she was Jessica.

"Yeah, he's all right. It's just that, you know, it's hard to meet other guys if one guy is always hanging around you." Lila took a sip of her diet soda and went on. "I mean, come on! Who wants to be tied down to one guy? You know what I mean?"

Elizabeth nodded. "Well, I'm sure you'll work it out. Lila. Listen, I wanted to—"

"Anyway," Lila interrupted, "I had a brilliant idea today. Maybe you could run a little item in the 'Eyes and Ears' column, you know, something like 'Who's the new hunk Lila Fowler's sneaking around with on weekends these days? Don't know his face, but the UCLA jacket gives us a clue. . . .' " She paused for a moment. "Well, what do you think, Liz?"

"You're going out with someone from UCLA?" Jessica hadn't mentioned anything about Lila having a new boyfriend. And Jessica was usually the first to know about Lila's ever-changing boyfriends, especially the older ones.

"Well . . ." Lila said, her eyes gleaming conspiratorially. "But we could make someone up— you know, use some athletic, gorgeous-sounding guy's name, describe him as a football player who's also a male model. Then John would really get the message."

Elizabeth smiled and shook her head. As the writer of the only gossip column in the school newspaper, Elizabeth often got requests to include information to help out certain couples. But she never honored these requests. "Sorry, Lila. That's not the 'Eyes and Ears' style. We report what's going on, we don't make things happen. You know that." She watched Lila as she pouted childishly. Lila wasn't used to not getting her way. Elizabeth still had to ask the question that was on her mind. She figured she would try to appeal to Lila's love of gossip. "But speaking of rumors, Lila, someone tells me you know the scoop about what Bruce

Patman is up to." She looked both ways and lowered her voice. "Like who he's interested in these days."

She's going to wonder why I'm asking her this, Elizabeth thought. Gossiping was the last thing Lila would expect from her.

Sure enough, Lila gave Elizabeth a quizzical look. "Why, Elizabeth? Are *you* interested in Bruce now?"

"Of course not. But I know someone who is. And Jessica mentioned that you knew Bruce had really fallen for some girl, so I just wondered if it was the same person."

"Well, Jessica must be mistaken. How would *I* know about Bruce's love life? She must have heard it some other place." Just then a group of girls sat down at the next table. Lila looked at Elizabeth and said, "Maybe she read about it in *The Oracle.*" Then she plunged into a conversation with the other girls, scooting her chair closer to them. She completely ignored Elizabeth.

Feeling even more frustrated than before, Elizabeth got up and gloomily put her lunch tray on the conveyor belt, her food completely untouched.

"Ooh, that little sneak!" Jessica said as she yanked open her locker after school. "She was just mad at you because you wouldn't print her story in your column—that's the only reason she wouldn't tell you. When Lila gets like that, you might as well forget about asking her for anything."

"But she did mention something about Bruce's new girlfriend to you, didn't she?"

"Liz, I could have sworn she did, but it was in the middle of a whole other big conversation. She said Bruce was bragging about some dynamite girl he was seeing—a tall, slender blond who's a senior. I mean it sure didn't *sound* like he was talking about Julie!" She unzipped her shoulder bag and plopped it on the ground. "Could you help me with this?"

Elizabeth helped Jessica take her books out of her shoulder bag and stuff her leotard and ballet shoes in. She wanted to talk more about Lila's rumor, but she knew there was really only one thing on Jessica's mind: getting to her audition on time.

"*Where* are my leg warmers?" Jessica said, panic creeping into her voice. "I know I brought them to school!"

"Take it easy, Jess. Let's just look carefully." Elizabeth dug underneath a pile of papers, then felt behind a jacket that was hanging on the rear hook. "Here they are." She gave them to Jessica and said, "Now, are you totally prepared? Do you need anything?"

"I did a triple pirouette this morning, Liz—that's all I care about. I feel wonderful!"

"Great! Are they just going to have you dance today?"

"Well, if they like me, they'll have me read from the script, too. Then if they like *that*, I'll have to do it all over again at the callback tomorrow."

"Did you get a chance to read through the play this week?"

"Oh, Liz, that's the least of my worries. I know how to read from a script. The dancing's the part I need to concentrate on."

"All right. You know what you're doing," Elizabeth said. "Now, knock 'em dead! I would say 'Break a leg,' but I'm afraid that you would. I'm sure you'll do fine, though."

Jessica impulsively threw her arms around her twin. "Thanks, Liz. You've been such a help this week. You are the *best* sister a girl could have!"

As Elizabeth watched Jessica hurry down the hallway toward the auditorium, she could feel her own heart begin to race, as if *she* were about to audition. She crossed her fingers for her sister.

"OK, you guys, get to work!" Bruce's voice boomed through the huge basement party room of the Patman house. "Remember, you aren't Phi Ep men yet!"

Josh kept running the vacuum cleaner over the pile carpeting. All around him the other pledges were working like crazy to set up the place, moving furniture off to the side, dusting, and doing all the other menial tasks Bruce had thought up. A few other brothers were looking on—Tom McKay, John Pfeifer, and Ronnie Edwards. None of them were bothering the pledges, but they weren't doing anything to help out, either. In fact, they were mostly eating, drinking, and generally making a mess wherever there was a clean area. Josh couldn't understand why all this had to be done the day *before* the party. Then it dawned on him: They were probably going to have to do it all over again tomorrow; that would really fit Bruce's twisted idea of pledge duties.

Bruce walked right in front of Josh's path, so close that Josh had to jerk the vacuum cleaner back out of his way, right into his own toes. "Excuse me, Bowen," Bruce said without looking at Josh. He walked over to where the carpet met the wall and pulled out a little dust ball.

"What's *this*?" he said, holding it up in front of Josh's face. "I thought the point was to get rid of funky substances like this. Isn't that right, Bowen?"

No matter how hard he tried, Josh couldn't get used to the wild swings in Bruce's behavior. Here he was being cruel again, after that apology Tuesday at Casey's Place. "Sorry, Bruce. I'll clean in between the cracks after I finish vacuuming."

Bruce raised the dust ball over Josh's head and let it fall into his hair. "Good. In the meantime, you can wear this little thinking cap to remind yourself." He turned so everyone else in the room could hear him. "And that goes for all of you! I see anybody taking shortcuts and you'll be doing the same thing tomorrow, understand? Do a good job today and you'll get one of the cushy jobs tomorrow—laying out the food and punch, putting up the decorations. You know, the easy stuff. You'll feel like you're in a sorority instead of big, bad Phi Epsilon."

The rest of the pledges laughed at Bruce's joke, but Josh ignored it and kept on working.

"What's the matter, Bowen?" Bruce said threateningly. "I don't hear you laughing."

Josh was clenching his teeth so hard, his jaw had begun to ache. He had to restrain the urge to pick up the vacuum cleaner like a baseball bat and give Bruce a whack on the rear end. Instead, he concentrated even harder on his vacuuming and pretended he hadn't heard Bruce.

"Oh, I see you're really into domestic work. You know, you'd make someone a good wife, Bowen!"

Again there was laughter from some of the other pledges—laughter that sounded forced to Josh, as if the guys were afraid of what would happen if they *didn't* laugh. But now Josh was fuming inside, and he couldn't hold it in any longer. "I don't think you're very funny, Bruce," he said, almost under his breath.

"What was that, pledge?" Bruce put his face inches away from Josh's. "Did I hear something?"

Josh turned off the vacuum cleaner and looked Bruce squarely in the eye. "I said, I don't think you're very funny." The shocked look on Bruce's face filled Josh with strength instead of fear. "In fact," he continued, "I think you've got a lousy sense of humor."

The room fell abruptly silent. Bruce's eyes burned into Josh's as he stepped even closer to him and began rolling up his sleeves. "Take it back," he ordered.

Josh felt everyone staring at him, waiting for a response. But he didn't say a word.

"I said, take it back, Bowen, or you're in big trouble."

Don't back down, Josh repeated to himself. *He's exactly the same size as you are.* Summoning up all his courage, Josh held his ground.

Suddenly Bruce gave Josh a push and sent him flying over the vacuum cleaner. Josh crashed into a bookcase, sending books showering down over him. With a catlike leap Bruce jumped on top of him.

"You asked for this, Bowen!" Bruce said through gritted teeth, grabbing Josh by the shirt. Josh tried to scramble to his feet, slipping on the fallen books.

Immediately Ronnie, Tom, and John rushed over. "Hey, come on, knock it off!" John said, pulling Bruce off Josh. "Have you guys gone crazy?"

As John held back Bruce's arms, Josh could hear him say, "Take it easy, Bruce. You're taking this thing too seriously. He's doing a good job."

Bruce tore away from John's grip and started to compose himself. Then John gave a hand signal to someone, who quickly turned on the stereo. "OK, you two, cool off!" he said as each pledge slowly headed back to his particular chore.

Bruce brushed off his pants and tried to put a calm expression on his face. But Josh could practically see the steam rise from him as he said in a cold, controlled voice, "You know, if it were up to me, Bowen, you wouldn't even be pledging. You just better be glad your brother was a member—and pray you can last through the rest of the pledging period!"

After that comment Josh turned on his heels and stormed out of the basement. He felt that if he spent one more second in the same room as Bruce, he would explode. Leaving the house, he took the keys out of his pocket, walked toward his blue Chevrolet, then parked in a long driveway that led to the Patmans' multicar garage. In front of Josh's car was Bruce's sleek black Porsche. Its license plate, 1BRUCE1, made him feel a wave of disgust. For a split second he felt like ramming his car into it. He climbed into his Chevy and started the engine.

At that moment he heard John Pfeifer call, "Hey, Bowen, wait!"

Josh pretended to ignore John, but John came right up and leaned into the window. "Listen, Josh," he said, "don't let Bruce get to you. Sometimes he gets a little crazy, but he doesn't mean half the things he says." He smiled. "Just remember, we're not all like that."

"I don't know, John," Josh answered. "What's it going to be like if I do join, and Bruce and I have to hang out together?"

"I'll let you in on a little secret. Bruce would kill me if he knew I was telling you this." John took a deep breath. "Now, I know Bruce pretty well. He doesn't really talk much—I mean, talk

73

about what's going on inside him—but he said something the other day I couldn't forget. He said he'd let himself get too soft, too vulnerable when he was going out with Regina. Somehow he thinks if he'd been tougher, he wouldn't be hurting so much."

"But that's—"

"Ridiculous. I know. You've got to understand that he's in bad shape. And when he sees you . . . well, I think you remind him of the nice guy he became around Regina. I have a feeling he's trying to, you know, toughen you up or something. I guess by being hard on you, in a way he's being hard on himself."

Josh nodded. He was a little confused by the suggestion that he had become Bruce's alter ego, but he also felt more sympathetic toward Bruce.

"Hey, listen," John said. "I guarantee Bruce will want to be your best friend as soon as you get in. Stick with it, OK? There's only a week left of pledging. Try not to take it so seriously. There are a bunch of us rooting for you."

"Thanks, John," Josh said.

"No problem. See you at the party tomorrow."

Josh backed down the long driveway, past the rolling front lawn of the Patman estate. At the end of the driveway was a row of tall pines, shielding the Spanish-style mansion from the

74

street. Josh turned into the street and drove through the quiet hill section of Sweet Valley.

As he drove, Josh tried to sort out all the thoughts that were jumbled in his mind. A minute ago he was ready to quit Phi Epsilon, but John's explanation had made Bruce seem a lot more human. *John's a good guy*, Josh realized. *It would be great to hang out with him.* With guys like John and Winston, Phi Epsilon would be a fun group, just the way Phil had said it would be. Maybe someday he and Bruce could even become friends. Still, there was something so untrustworthy about Bruce. One minute he was acting as if he owned the world, and the next minute he had enough warmth and charm to make Julie fall for him.

The idea of Julie going to the party with Bruce made Josh uneasy. Julie was such a good person, and so innocent. Was Bruce really interested in her, or did he want to use her? That last thought made his blood boil. *If he does anything to hurt her, he'll be sorry,* he thought.

The strength of Josh's feelings for Julie surprised him. He felt protective of her, as if she were his best friend—or his girlfriend. He'd never thought of her that way before, but somehow it made sense. It seemed natural. Maybe their friendship had grown into something deeper without his realizing it. But how did

Julie feel about him? She seemed more interested in Bruce these days than an old friend like him, Josh thought.

He turned onto a street that took him past Sweet Valley High. Out of the corner of his eye he saw Elizabeth walking out the front door.

He turned in and pulled up beside her. "Hi, Elizabeth. How come you're still here? Want a ride?"

"Oh, hi, Josh. Sure!" She walked around and got in the passenger side. "Jessica's staying late today, so she's driving our car. I was just wishing her good luck for her audition, and then I stopped by the *Oracle* office. What are you doing?"

Josh sighed as he pulled away from the curb. "Good question. I feel like I've just been through an hour of torture at Bruce's parents' house—or should I say mansion. He made all the pledges clean the party room."

"I'm surprised he didn't have the servants do it."

Josh laughed. "Then there wouldn't be a way to make the pledges miserable. Besides, his parents are away, so he can do whatever he wants with the place. Did you hear he asked Julie to the party?"

Elizabeth nodded. "And he asked someone else, too."

"What?"

"Well, that's what I heard. I just can't understand what's going on.'

"No kidding," Josh said. He felt his anger for Bruce begin to rise up again.

"I just feel so torn, Josh. Julie is my friend, and I don't want to meddle in her personal life. I already tried to warn her about Bruce, and she got really upset." She sighed. "But I feel this incredible urge to let her know that Bruce asked someone else and that she may not be his only date. I just don't know what to do."

Josh had an idea. "I know what to do and where to go," he said firmly. "We're going over to Julie's right now. Rumor or not, we're going to tell her."

Seven

Sometimes the Fantaisie Impromptu was impossible, and this afternoon was one of those times. Julie's fingers felt as if they had lead weights tied to them. She let out a big sigh and flopped her arms down on the piano, causing a loud, ugly chord to resound throughout the living room. She couldn't stop thinking about Bruce and Friday night.

Come on, snap out of it, she said to herself. She didn't want to think about anybody or anything right now. The most important thing was her music. Adjusting herself on the piano bench, Julie poised her fingertips just above the keys.

But just as she was about to strike the first notes, the doorbell sounded.

"I'll get it!" she shouted so her father could hear her in his practice room. She went to the front door and pulled it open.

"Elizabeth and Josh, hi! Come on in," she said. "This is a nice surprise."

"Liked that last chord, Julie!" Josh said jokingly. "Some modern composer or your own improvisation?"

Julie laughed. "It's an original piece, the I'm Tired of Practicing Today Impromptu."

"I know that tune," Josh nodded. "I hear my mother play it every now and then."

Elizabeth and Julie smiled. For a moment there was a tense silence, and Julie had a feeling there was something on their minds. "So, what brings you two here?" she asked. "Oh! How can I be so rude? Would you like something to drink?"

"No, thanks, Julie," Josh said. "We—uh—stopped by to tell you something."

"Sure, OK." Julie gestured toward the couch. "Have a seat." As she sat on the piano bench, facing them, she wondered what they wanted to talk about. From the somber looks on her friends' faces, she could tell it was something serious.

"Well," Elizabeth began. "I don't know how to say this, or even *if* I should say this, but there's a rumor going around—"

"And we want to stress that it's a *rumor*," Josh added.

"That's right, nobody seems to know for sure. . . ."

Oh, please, get on with it, Julie thought.

Elizabeth sighed. "Lila Fowler, who, as we all know, thinks she knows everything that goes on in Sweet Valley, told Jessica that Bruce Patman asked another girl to the Phi Ep party."

Julie's first reaction was to laugh. "That's silly," she said. "Lila must have heard wrong. She probably heard that he asked *me* to the party."

"That's just it. The only detail Jessica heard is that she was a tall, blond senior. That doesn't exactly sound like you."

Julie slumped down on the piano bench. "Someone tall and blond? Are you sure?"

"That's what she said. Now, this could be total nonsense, Julie, and maybe we're just worrying about nothing. But I've known for a long time that Bruce Patman can't always be trusted. I mean, I don't want to accuse him, but I wouldn't be all that surprised if he asked two of you to the party."

"Well, *I* don't mind accusing him behind his back," Josh said, an angry edge to his voice. "The more I have to deal with him, the less I see to like about him."

Julie nodded slowly. She tried to keep the anger and hurt from welling up inside her, but

80

it was no use. "I can't believe it," she murmured. "How could he!"

Out of the corner of her eye she caught a glimpse of Elizabeth looking nervously at Josh.

"Why isn't this senior going to the party with him?" Julie continued. "Did she turn him down? Am I her backup or something? His substitute date? Or is he just using me to make her jealous?"

"I knew this would happen," Josh said, shaking his head. He went over to Julie and sat next to her. "Listen, you shouldn't jump to conclusions like that." He put his arm around her shoulder and smiled. "Bruce may be completely on the level. There may not even *be* another girl. I mean, it's no surprise that any guy would like you. But Liz and I just wanted to be the ones to tell you about the rumor."

"Remember, no one's forcing you to go to this party if you don't want to, Julie," Elizabeth said. "But if you do, you should just—you know, look out."

Suddenly Julie felt all her defenses falling away. Tears started clouding her vision. "I feel so confused. Bruce seemed so—so honest. Not at all like the horrible guy you're describing. Oh, Josh, I just don't understand!" She buried her head in Josh's broad chest and began to cry softly.

81

Josh stroked her hair gently. "I'm sorry, Julie. Maybe we shouldn't have told you anything."

"No. No," Julie replied, wiping her eyes. "I'm glad you did. Really. It's better that I know. It would hurt more if something bad happened later on, and you guys hadn't told me about Bruce, even if it is just a rumor. But I'm going to need some time to think about all this."

Elizabeth got up from the couch. "OK, I guess we'd better leave you alone, then," she said. "Promise you'll call if you need to talk."

"You can always call me, too," Josh said.

Julie nodded as she opened the front door. "Yeah. Thanks, guys."

After Elizabeth and Josh left, Julie sat back down at the piano. With two fingers of her right hand, she lazily played a childish melody. Her mind raced. A strong voice inside her said that she should forget about Bruce, that he obviously wasn't worth the trouble. But then she thought of his beautiful eyes, his soothing voice, and she imagined how great it would feel to walk into the party with his arm around her.

Finally it all came down to one thing: *Bruce could like someone else, but I'm the one who's going to the party with him. She smiled. And even if we never go out together again, it'll probably be a night I'll always remember.*

* * *

82

"OK, DeeDee," Mr. Jaworski said. "See if you can round up the guys trying out for Grandpa. I think some of them are out in the hall."

As the drama club president stood up to walk to the back of the auditorium, she spotted Jessica sitting behind her. "You've still got a few minutes, Jessica," DeeDee whispered with a friendly wink. "Hang in there!"

Jessica propped her feet up on the seat in front of her. With each passing minute she was starting to feel more and more anxious. It seemed as though she had been waiting there for hours. *Why is Mr. Jaworski auditioning everyone in the world before me?* she wondered. *Doesn't he know a dancer's body gets stiff if she sits around too much?*

Quietly Jessica got up and sneaked out of the auditorium into the lobby. By now the rest of the school had gone home, which meant she had the whole place to herself to practice her moves. She sailed into a combination, looking at her reflection in the school's trophy case. *This is it*, she thought. *This is the best I can do.* She planted her feet, focused on a trophy in the case, and did a double pirouette. Finishing in a perfect third position, arms exactly right, she smiled proudly. *And it's really not too bad.*

Just then she heard Mr. Jaworski's booming voice call out, "OK, where are my Essies? Come on, kids, it's getting late."

Essie. That was the name of Jessica's part. She froze momentarily. Her skin tingled with nervousness, and she took a deep breath and tried to calm herself. Then all of a sudden she felt an incredible surge of positive energy. *If I'm not ready for this, nobody is,* she thought, her confidence returning. She couldn't keep from grinning as she threw open the door and raced into the auditorium.

"I'm here, Mr. Jaworski!" she called out. "I'll be right on stage!"

Mr. Jaworski turned around with a harried smile. "Sorry this took so long, Jessica. We had a few more boys than we expected. Why don't you have a seat? You'll be second."

Second? Jessica thought. She felt all the adrenaline drain right back out of her. *What's going on here? Nobody said there'd be anyone else trying out.* Slowly she sat down and watched as DeeDee popped her head out from stage left.

"I found her," DeeDee said. "She was practicing in the orchestra room."

"All right," Mr. Jaworski answered. "Is she ready to do her combination?"

"Yep!" DeeDee said and disappeared backstage.

Jessica watched the curtains begin to ripple as someone behind them groped around for the opening onto the stage.

Suddenly the rippling stopped, and the other auditioner stepped through.

It was Danielle.

Jessica felt her heart skip a beat. Her stomach began doing flip-flops, and every last ounce of hope deserted her. *DeeDee betrayed me*, she thought, watching her friend take a seat next to Mr. Jaworski near the front of the stage. Then something dawned on her: DeeDee had never actually *told* her no one else was trying out. Jessica had just assumed it. She sank further into her seat, full of hurt and anger—and the knowledge she had brought it all on herself. She wondered how many other girls who were sitting in the auditorium were auditioning for Essie.

Danielle walked gracefully downstage, wearing the white leotard Jessica and Lila had seen her buy. Her hair shone beautifully in the stage lights, and she gave Mr. Jaworski a smile that radiated to the back of the auditorium. *She must have practiced that phony smile all week,* Jessica thought.

"OK, Danielle," Mr. Jaworski said warmly. "We're all ready for you. You can have a minute to get used to the stage if you'd like, work out any jitters."

Danielle's eyes twinkled as she laughed. "Oh, I'm not jittery, Mr. Jaworksi. I've been through this kind of thing a lot!"

Modest, isn't she? Jessica thought to herself.

"Good! Then we'll start right away. First I'd like you to do a simple combination of your own. Nothing fancy, just something to show me that you know what you're doing. Then after you're through, I'll give you some directions, OK?"

"OK!" Danielle answered enthusiastically. She took center stage and paused, head held high, as if waiting for a whole audience to focus on her. Then Danielle launched into the most complicated ballet routine Jessica had ever seen a high-school student perform. It looked like a solo she had seen in a professional production of *Romeo and Juliet*. As Danielle pranced about the stage, doing flawless jetés, Jessica left her seat and ran back into the hallway.

She felt gripped with panic. *Some simple combination,* she thought. *I'm going to look ridiculous in comparison! I should just leave before I humiliate myself. This part isn't that important.*

Through the closed door Jessica could hear the muffled sound of a conversation between Mr. Jaworski and Danielle. *What am I going to do when he calls my name?* she thought. *If I go on stage, I'll embarrass myself—and if I don't, everyone will know I chickened out. How will I explain that?* She opened the door a crack and peeked in. Danielle was still onstage, doing another combination—only this time she looked different. Her pirouettes were wobbly, and her positions were awkward. And each time she made a mistake she made a weird face, as if to say, "What am I doing up here?"

Jessica was amazed. Danielle was really falling apart! *Not jittery, huh?* she thought. *This isn't even going to be close.* Jessica stepped back in the auditorium, determined to win the part.

"Thank you very much, Danielle, that was great. We'll let you know what we decide. OK, where's Jessica? I think we've let her wait long enough."

Danielle walked off into the wings as Jessica climbed onto the stage. She walked slowly across to stage center, making sure that her new leotard would have its maximum effect. Then she turned and flashed her brightest, most winning smile at Mr. Jaworski. "Gee, I don't know how I can follow *that* up, but I'll sure give it a try!"

She started slowly, doing a few simple exercises that went through the positions. Then she built up to an arabesque and went into a combination she had practiced. Everything was going perfectly until she came to a simple kick. She lifted her right leg and immediately felt a slight pull where she had strained it. With a loud *whomp* she landed on the floor—on her rear end, as usual.

"Are you all right?" Mr. Jaworski asked, getting up from his seat.

Jessica thought quickly. "Uh, that's my famous grand floppé!" she said, making the name up on the spot. "Did you like it?"

Mr. Jaworski's face lit up into a smile. "Grand floppé," he said, chuckling. "That's funny."

Jessica scrambled up off the stage floor. She had managed to joke her way out of that, but she could still redeem herself with her grand finale, a double pirouette. She prepared herself and breathed deeply. *I've got to make this good*, she thought. And then an idea crossed her mind. Why not make it a triple? That would really dazzle them.

She bent her knees extra deeply and gave herself more of a push than usual. She spun once, twice, and then found herself stumbling backward on the stage, her arms flailing. She ended upstage, with her back to the auditorium and her feet wide apart.

Quickly she whirled around to see DeeDee and Mr. Jaworski looking at each other with a smile. From the wings she heard a muffled giggle, and she looked over to see Danielle covering her mouth. At that moment Jessica wanted to melt into the floor. Not only was she more awful than she expected, but everyone was laughing at her! She could feel tears forming in the corners of her eyes.

Mr. Jaworski came to the side of the stage. "Wonderful, Jessica," he said. "I was going to give you a few directions, but we're running late, and we have some other girls to audition. In fact, I'm not even going to ask any of the dancers to read today."

Jessica valiantly kept herself from crying. She sat down by the edge of the stage, ready to go home and forget the whole thing.

But Mr. Jaworski wasn't finished. "Anyway, I can give you directions tomorrow. That is, if you're free to come to callbacks after school. Can you make it?"

Jessica couldn't believe her ears. He hadn't asked Danielle to come back. She just stared at him in disbelief.

Her confusion must have showed, because he grinned and said, "That's right, I think you might be right for this part, Jessica. Just make sure you read the play carefully if you haven't already, will you?"

Jessica felt too numb to do anything but nod. But when she walked out of the auditorium toward her locker, she was so happy she couldn't even feel the floor beneath her feet.

Eight

"What do you mean, the sports column is too short?" Penny Ayala, editor in chief of *The Oracle*, said. "Pad it! Use some of the filler we have!"

Elizabeth could hardly concentrate on finishing her own column. All around her, people were talking about what *they* still had to do for the next edition of *The Oracle*.

"I've finally got a headline for the music review: 'The Surf Boys Go Solo; McGaffin Excels.' "

"It took you two days to come up with that?"

"The picture of Mr. Marks is cropped wrong!"

"Where's the 'Eyes and Ears' column?"

It was a typical deadline day in the *Oracle* office—loud voices and short tempers. But this was a little worse than usual, and Elizabeth knew why. Not only was it a Friday, but also the Phi Epsilon party was going to start in a few hours, and everyone wanted to get the paper done even quicker than usual so they could go home and get ready.

"It's right here, Penny!" Elizabeth called out. "You can have it in two minutes."

Elizabeth quickly typed out the last two lines and pulled her paper out of the typewriter. She was in a rush, too. If she didn't get to the auditorium to wish Jessica luck in her callback, she'd never hear the end of it.

She collated the typewritten pages and quickly straightened up the mess on her desk. Just then Olivia Davidson, the arts editor, came by and placed a sheet of paper on the desk. "This is for you, Elizabeth," she said. "It's been sitting under a pile of papers on my desk for a while. Somebody must have put it there by mistake."

Elizabeth glanced at it. On top of the page someone had typed the words "Submitted for the 'Eyes and Ears' column. Phi Epsilon Party Scoop!" Below it was a paragraph full of names. She didn't read it, but she caught a glimpse of some familiar names—Tom McKay, Amy Sutton, Winston, Danielle. "Well, it's a little late now," she told Olivia. "The party's tonight, and this will be ancient history by the time the paper comes out. Anyway, I've got to go!"

She tossed her column onto Penny's desk and rushed out into the hallway. When she got to the auditorium, Jessica had already gone inside. Elizabeth opened the door quickly and saw her sister doing stretching exercises in the area behind the seats.

"Oh, Liz, you're here!" Jessica whispered.

"I just wanted to wish you—"

"Shh. They're starting. Let's go into the hallway."

They tiptoed out the door. But before Elizabeth could say a word, a voice called out, "Good luck, Jessica!"

Elizabeth and Jessica turned to see Danielle walking toward them. "I didn't get a chance to congratulate you yesterday," Danielle continued with a smile. "They really liked your audition."

"Thank you, Danielle," Jessica said. Then she added nonchalantly, "Your audition was wonderful. I thought you'd be my toughest competition."

Danielle laughed. "Well, to tell you the truth, I was really using this audition as a warm-up for my L.A. Ballet audition. I'm not sure I could have fit the play into my schedule anyway." She tossed back her silken blond hair. "Besides, now I can see my date before the Phi Epsilon party starts. See you two there, I hope. Bye!"

Elizabeth watched Danielle's tall, slinky form

disappear down the hallway. Even with flats on, she towered over most of the girls she passed by. Suddenly Elizabeth thought about how Lila had described Bruce's date to Jessica, the one who had supposedly turned down his invitation to the party. She was a tall, blond senior. The description fit Danielle perfectly, although she had just said that she would be going to the party. Could Bruce really have been rotten enough to invite *two* dates to the party?

Jessica threw her head up in the air and put on a breathy-sounding voice, in a perfect imitation of Danielle. " 'You see, *I* was simply too *good* for the drama club production. They just knew I would embarrass everyone else on stage!' The truth is, Liz, her audition fell apart even worse than mine did!"

Elizabeth was thinking about the party article that had been submitted to her column. Danielle's name had been in it, and Elizabeth planned to look at the article again as soon as she left Jessica. She had an urge to tell Jessica what she suspected, but now wasn't the right time. Instead, she just smiled and said, "Listen, don't think of anyone but yourself. Just go in there and get that part!"

"Thanks, Liz. I'll let you know all about it at the party. Keep your fingers crossed. Bye."

Elizabeth ran back to the newspaper office. She found the article exactly where she had left it. She skimmed it quickly, looking for the sentence with Danielle's name.

What she read confirmed her worst fears: "Bruce Patman may really be the host with the most! Not only is he giving one of Sweet Valley High's biggest parties, but he's been seen lately with beautiful blond Danielle Alexander. Will she be his date for the party?"

This had gone too far. She had to tell Julie, Elizabeth thought. She rushed toward the office door, but another thought forced her to slow down. *It doesn't actually say Danielle's going tonight. And even if it did, it's still only a rumor. What if Danielle is really going with someone else? After all, Lila did tell Jessica that Bruce had been turned down.*

Elizabeth put her hand on the doorknob, trying to figure out what would be fairest for Julie. Finally she made up her mind. She had told Julie everything all along, and she might as well continue.

"Elizabeth! You're here!" Penny Ayala's voice rang out behind her. "Listen, you want to count words on that column? I'm not sure it'll fit the space."

"Uh, sure, Penny!" Elizabeth shouted above the noise in the room. "I just have to step out for a second!"

Julie had mentioned she would be practicing in the orchestra room during last period. Elizabeth got there just in time to see Julie leaving the room and heading for the front door of the school.

"Julie, wait up!" she called out.

"Elizabeth," Julie answered, spinning around. "You got out of your newspaper meeting early. Going home?"

"Uh, no. Actually, I'm not finished yet. I have to get back. But I wanted to tell you something—"

"First I have to ask *you* something. Can I go over to the party with you tonight?"

"Well, Jeffrey's driving me, but I'm sure he won't mind giving you a lift. What about Bruce?"

"Well, that's just it. I'm not going to the party with Bruce."

Elizabeth couldn't have been happier. *She finally came to her senses*, she thought. "But you still want to go, alone?"

Julie looked puzzled for a moment, then laughed. "Oh! I didn't mean we're not going to be dates. I just meant he's not going to take me. You see, he was going to come by my place at seven-thirty, but he told me today that he has to get his house set up and that he needs to do some last-minute errands. So he wants me to meet him there."

Elizabeth's mood suddenly changed as she had an unpleasant thought: Maybe Bruce had asked Julie to the party so that he'd have someone to be with early in the evening while Danielle was at the callback. And now that she wasn't called back, she and Bruce were free to get together before the party!

"Um, OK," Elizabeth said. "After I finish up at *The Oracle*, I'll call Jeffrey and then let you know what time we'll be picking you up. We're giving Enid a ride, too."

"That's great, it'll be fun to go together. Thanks—see you later!"

Elizabeth opened her mouth to call out and stop Julie as she ran out the door, but she decided against it. Julie looked too happy to have her evening spoiled, especially if Elizabeth was wrong about Danielle.

With a sigh Elizabeth walked down the hall, hoping she had made the right decision.

"Now, one last thing before we get started," Mr. Jaworski said to the group of auditioners. "You're all here because I think you're right for the roles in this show. A lot has to do with your talent—and you all have that in abundance! But there are other things that go into selecting actors—whether they look the part, how they react to their fellow performers . . ."

Jessica looked at the other girl who was called back for Essie. *Kind of goony-looking,* she thought. *How strange he would pick someone like that over Danielle. She must be an amazing dancer.*

"So this callback will be lasting quite some time. You'll all be reading alone and with others. Now, I know some of you have a certain unbreakable social engagement, so I'd like to go through this as fast as possible. OK, since our Essies were last yesterday, I'd like to see them first. Jessica, why don't you step onstage. The rest of you can wait in the hallway."

Jessica was a little shocked to be first, but she felt strong and ready. Quickly she took a comb out of her bag and ran it through her hair. Then she went onto the stage, trying to slink as sexily as possible.

Mr. Jaworski came to the edge of the stage. "OK, Jess, it was clear from your audition that you know how to dance ballet. But this play requires a very *special* kind of dancing, as you know from reading the part, right?"

Jessica nodded. *What he doesn't know won't hurt him*, she thought.

"Which is why I was so pleased at the mistakes you made on purpose. It's so important to know how to do ballet right if you want to do it wrong. I *loved* your grand floppé. Now, I want you to do the same combination you did yesterday, only this time make it *really* awful. Don't be afraid to clown it up, OK?" He sat down again in his seat. "Whenever you're ready."

Jessica was stunned. *Was this some kind of weird relaxation exercise?* she wondered. Slowly she went into her combination, trying not to lift her leg as high, shaking on her arabesque. *So this is why Danielle looked so bad the second time I saw her, after Mr. Jaworski talked to her!*

"That's it, but take it even further. Pretend for a minute you've taken ballet all your life, but your left arm and leg have been switched with your right. So all you can do is try harder and harder—kick your leg *too* high, flail your arms like windmills!"

I get it, Jessica thought. *This is his idea of a test. He wants to see if I can follow directions.* She smiled to herself. *OK, Mr. Jaworski, you want a good actress? Watch this!*

Jessica followed his direction. She did a jeté and bent her leg ridiculously in the back. Then she went into a series of fouetté turns and staggered around the stage as if she were dizzy. She ended with a pirouette that led into an awkward tap-dance routine. It was actually kind of fun. Mr. Jaworski burst out laughing, as did DeeDee, who was sitting next to him and giving Jessica the thumbs-up sign.

"Terrific, Jessica, that's exactly what I had in mind. You really have a handle on the character." He gave her a set of photocopied sheets. "I want you to read one of Essie's scenes now. Take it into the hallway and look it over. And when you read for me, keep the same spirit! Remember, this character is *funny*. She *thinks*

98

she's a ballerina, but in truth she's the worst dancer you could possibly imagine!"

Jessica's hand went weak as she took the papers from him. She felt as if someone had thrown a cold bucket of water in her face. "The worst dancer . . ." she repeated.

"That's right. If you do this right, you'll have the audience laughing the minute you step on stage."

Jessica was horrified. *This is a comic role, not the romantic lead,* she realized. *He wants me to make a total fool of myself!* She gulped and tried to smile at Mr. Jaworski. Suddenly her dreams of sweeping gracefully across the stage in front of an adoring audience had just gone up in smoke.

Nine

"OK, this is the last stop on our scenic tour, the Patman mansion!" Jeffrey's smooth voice called out as he parked the car on Valley Coast Drive. "Everybody out. Fares will be collected from all passengers before leaving the vehicle! No exceptions and no discounts."

Elizabeth laughed and playfully pushed Jeffrey out the car door. From the backseat Enid reached out to help her, and Julie just giggled.

Jeffrey sprang out of the car and then leaned back in, his palm outstretched. He blinked his eyes with mock earnestness and said, "Hey, you didn't think you'd be getting a free ride, did you? Keeping up this beautiful automobile is expensive, you know."

"I know," Elizabeth said with a giggle, "especially if you don't have the keys!" She pulled them out of the ignition and slapped them into Jeffrey's open hand.

Jeffrey sighed. "Oh, well, so much for my business skills. I guess I'll never become a tycoon."

"Too bad," Enid said with a wry smile. "That means you'll never live in this neighborhood."

Julie looked around as she stepped out of the car. She had driven through the hill section of Sweet Valley before but had never really stopped to admire its stunning beauty. Spanish-style estates lined the curving streets, each one shielded by palms and junipers and surrounded by a huge expanse of perfectly kept lawn. Some of them were set so far back from the road, you couldn't see them.

"Which one is Bruce's?" Julie asked.

"We're right in front of it," Enid replied, pointing up the Patmans' long, winding driveway. "I know, we should have told you to bring hiking shoes for the walk, right?"

Julie looked up the driveway. The Patmans' house was perched like a castle on the very top of a hill. "Amazing," she said, under her breath.

Jeffrey tucked Elizabeth's arm in his. Then, putting on an exaggerated heroic expression, he looked around at Julie and Enid and said, "Stay right by me, girls. You can't be too safe in this neighborhood!"

Julie rolled her eyes and laughed, as did Enid and Elizabeth. She couldn't believe her good fortune—a date with Bruce, and a great new set of friends, all in the same week! She could feel herself practically skipping as they walked toward the mansion.

Jeffrey knocked on the door, and immediately it flew open. "Welcome to the Phi Epsilon fun festival!" a high-pitched voice exclaimed. Jeffrey, Elizabeth, and Enid all burst out laughing. Standing behind them, Julie couldn't see who it was at first, but when she did, she felt a twinge of pity. It was Josh, wearing a ludicrous long blond wig.

"They didn't tell me they were going to import beautiful girls for this party," Jeffrey said. "I would have left Liz at home."

Elizabeth gave Jeffrey a good-natured kick. "I'm sorry, Josh," she said. "But you are about the ugliest woman I've ever seen!"

"Thank you," answered Josh brightly. Then, under his breath, he whispered, "If I don't break character, I can take this hideous thing off in an hour." Switching to his female voice, he said, "Come on in."

As they walked into the foyer Julie said softly to Josh, "You must be dying for pledge period to be over."

"Only another week," Josh answered. He shrugged and went back to the door, smiling.

He's taking these pledge duties so seriously, Julie thought. For a moment it occurred to her that maybe he actually *enjoyed* it.

Julie joined the other three as they went down to the basement, where the party was already in full swing. There must have been fifty students, some with dates, some without. The furniture had been cleared off to the sides to make a dancing area in the middle. In a dark alcove there were some soft chairs and couches. Most of the couches were empty, but Julie could see the silhouettes of two or three couples sitting there, talking intimately. A tingle went through her when she imagined that she and Bruce might end up there later.

"There's food and drink in the back room. Help yourself," said a voice on Julie's left. She turned to see a boy wearing a hat made out of plastic fruit.

"Thanks," she answered, trying to stifle a laugh. She realized that Josh wasn't the only one being made a fool of. This pledge looked even sillier than Josh did! In fact, the room was full of pledges in weird outfits. One was wearing a propeller cap, another a fright mask, another a three-piece suit that looked about two sizes too small. And while the brothers were enjoying the party, the pledges ran around doing all the work—cleaning up, changing the CDs, putting out the food and drink.

Julie kept looking around until she spotted Bruce talking to Ronnie Edwards off in a corner. In his European-style cotton sweater, crisply pressed chinos, and brown loafers, Bruce looked incredibly handsome. A deep dimple creased his cheek as he laughed at something Ronnie said.

As she nervously walked toward him, Julie could feel herself wanting to believe in him, to trust him. But it was so hard to do. She tried to look nonchalant as she announced, "I'm here, Bruce! Great party!"

"Oh! Hi, Julie!" Bruce said, flashing a rakish smile. "I've been waiting for you!"

Ronnie gave them both a rather sly grin and walked away, leaving Julie and Bruce alone.

"I *love* your house," Julie said.

"Yeah, it's not bad," Bruce replied with a self-satisfied smirk. "Have you taken a tour?"

"Of course not. I haven't had a tour guide," Julie said coyly. She surprised herself with the way she was talking to him. Her tongue-tying shyness seemed to have disappeared for the moment.

"Oh, right," Bruce answered. "Well, let me start with the game room."

Bruce led her through a short hallway and into a large room full of couples. Some were gathered around a pool table, others were playing pinball, and still others were concentrating on video games on a twenty-six-inch display terminal.

"Fantastic," Julie said.

"Yeah," Bruce said smugly. "Nobody ever gets bored around here."

Julie didn't know what to say next. "Uh, do you want to play some pinball?"

Bruce chuckled. "No, I have other things in mind for tonight." He looked at Julie with a lopsided smile. "But hey, the tour has just begun."

Julie felt scared and excited as they headed up the stairs. She followed him out through a sliding glass door on the first floor.

The view over the sloping hill was breathtaking. Off to the left a tennis court had been cut into the hill. Just below it was an Olympic-size swimming pool.

"Like it?" Bruce asked.

"Wonderful," Julie answered. "Too bad I didn't bring my bathing suit."

Bruce turned back to the house. "It's fun to come out here at two in the morning and go skinny-dipping," he observed.

Again a shiver ran up Julie's spine. She was getting the feeling Bruce was going to be full of surprises that evening.

Bruce led Julie through the various ground-floor rooms of the house—the two living rooms, the enormous kitchen with a pantry the size of a garage, the home-entertainment room with a floor-projection TV.

After the last room, he guided Julie up the stairs to the second floor. "Not that much up here"—he paused with her at the top landing and looked deeply into her eyes—"except for the bedrooms."

Julie held her breath as Bruce opened the door to his bedroom. There was a gorgeous mahogany four-poster bed. One wall was covered with photos of Bruce in tennis and track team gear. A glassed-in case against another wall held several trophies and plaques, and a huge glossy poster of a Porsche just like Bruce's covered the third wall.

"This is where I spend a lot of my time," Bruce said with a chuckle. "The bed is an antique my mom picked up."

"Nice," Julie commented, not sure what to say.

Bruce seemed to hesitate, and Julie had the urge to bolt down the stairs. But Bruce simply closed the door and asked her to follow him back down to the party.

Julie was relieved. Maybe Elizabeth and Josh had thrown too much of a scare into her where Bruce was concerned. He came across as a bit of a flirt, but he seemed to be a gentleman after all.

As Elizabeth moved to the beat of the music, she realized she hadn't seen Julie in an hour. She had seen Julie walk away with Bruce, but then she'd lost track of her. Elizabeth hoped her friend was having a good time.

She tossed her hair back and smiled at Jeffrey, who was dancing in his athletic way. He wasn't exactly light on his feet, Elizabeth thought, but he was very sexy. As Elizabeth danced, all the faces around her became blurs that moved up and down and around as she did: Jeffrey, Enid, Amy Sutton and her date, Bruce, Danielle . . .

Bruce and Danielle! Suddenly Elizabeth stopped dancing. In a dark corner near the CD player, Bruce had his arm against the wall and was smiling at Danielle as she talked animatedly to him. His eyes darted around the room from time to time, as if he were hoping no one would see him. At one point he laughed at something Danielle said, and she put her fingers gently over his mouth. He looked across the room and seemed to see something. Quickly he nestled Danielle's chin in the palm of his hand, gave her a kiss, and walked away.

Elizabeth turned to see where he was going.

With horror she realized what was happening. He was going to meet Julie, who was approaching him with a lovesick smile on her face.

I've got to do something, Elizabeth thought. But Bruce and Julie were dancing now; there was no way Elizabeth could talk to her. All she could do was hope that Julie had paid attention to her warnings.

"Hey, are you OK?" Jeffrey asked.

"Yes—fine," Elizabeth answered, forcing a smile.

She caught a glimpse of Jessica over by the punch bowl. She was standing all alone and glumly sipping a cup of punch.

Uh-oh. Bad news about the audition, Elizabeth thought. "Uh, Jeffrey, why don't you dance with Enid for a while? She's all alone, and I want to sit out this next one."

"Sure," Jeffrey said. "No problem. I saw Jessica, too." Elizabeth smiled and squeezed his hand. She had told him about Jessica's audition, and she could tell he knew what was going on.

Jessica barely acknowledged her sister's presence when she came over. "Hey, don't worry about it, Jess," Elizabeth said. "It was only a dumb little play. You'll get another chance."

Jessica just nodded and took another sip of punch.

"Everyone faces rejection once in a while, you know," Elizabeth continued. "You're still a pretty terrific person. I'd want you to be in *my* play."

Jessica shook her head. "I wasn't rejected."

"You weren't? You mean you got the part?"

Jessica nodded.

"Well, that's *fantastic!* Congratulations!"

"I guess so. . . ."

"What's wrong, Jess? I thought you'd be really excited. Did something bad happen?"

"I don't think I want to do it, Liz."

"What? You've been working yourself to death all week for this!"

"I know, I know." Jessica turned away and flopped down into a canvas director's chair. "But the part is a lot different than I thought it would be." She sighed. "It's a *comedy* part, Liz. I'm supposed to dance so badly that the audience laughs at me!"

Elizabeth knelt down to Jessica. She could see that her twin's ego was bruised, but it was partly her own fault. If Jessica had only read the play beforehand, she would have known what the part was like.

"I know what you're thinking," Jessica said. "I should have read the play, right?"

"Well, no, Jess. I mean—"

Jessica sighed. "Yes, you were. And you were

right, Liz. It's just that there was just so much to do . . .''

Jessica went on, but Elizabeth found it hard to concentrate. She had her eye on Bruce and Julie. A slow song had started, and Julie rested her head on Bruce's shoulder as they danced.

After a few moments, Bruce stopped dancing and whispered something to Julie. A wide smile spread across her face, and she nodded dreamily.

Then, as Elizabeth watched with disbelieving eyes, Bruce took her hand and led her to the dark alcove in back—the alcove where several couples were locked in passionate embraces.

Ten

"I think it'll be much more comfortable for us back here," Bruce said with a sensuous gleam in his eye.

Julie looked around the alcove. It was hard to see much of anything besides the outlines of other people who were already comfortably sitting on the couches. Julie turned to Bruce. "Doesn't seem like there's anywhere to sit."

Bruce ran his fingers through her hair. "Don't forget, this is my house. I'll find room for us." He led her by the hand to a far corner of the alcove where a long leather couch faced away from the rest.

"Here we are, nice and private," he said. Slowly the two of them sank to the couch. Bruce smiled seductively and wrapped his arm around her.

Suddenly it dawned on Julie where she was, what she was doing. She hoped she could stay calm and fool Bruce into thinking she wasn't new at this kind of thing.

Bruce didn't say anything for a few minutes. Instead, he ran his fingers gently through Julie's hair. "There's something about red hair," Bruce said quietly. "Something so—so hot and fiery."

"Oh, a lot of girls have hair like this," Julie said bashfully.

"As far as I can see, there aren't any other girls in this room who do," Bruce answered. He moved closer to her, shifting the cushion in such a way that Julie couldn't help leaning toward him—and right into his arms.

"Oops, sorry," Julie said. She was glad the alcove was dark so that he couldn't see that she was blushing.

"Sorry about what? I think this is a much better position, don't you?"

Julie fidgeted a bit, trying to sit upright. "I—uh, feel like I'm sinking to one side."

"Hey, no problem! I know just the way to relieve that." With a firm but gentle pull he drew her closer to him, so that her head nestled against his broad chest. "There, now we're both feeling just right. . . ."

Julie had to admit it felt good to be so close to

Bruce. The beat of his heart through his sweater was rhythmic and soothing.

"Mmm. I could just sit here all night," Bruce said with a deep sigh.

"With this gorgeous, mysterious redhead who has seen my whole house but hasn't told me a thing about herself."

Just when Julie was afraid Bruce was going to go too far, he said something romantic and considerate. It was getting harder and harder for Julie to remember Elizabeth's and Josh's warnings. She was really beginning to trust him.

"Are you really interested, Bruce? I mean, it's not like I've led the world's most fascinating life."

"All I care about is that *you've* lived it," he said sweetly. "That makes it fascinating to me."

Julie began talking about herself. She said things she would never dream about saying to a boy, for fear he might become too bored—about her love for music, about her mother, her sister.

Bruce listened patiently, gently running his fingers through her hair and asking questions.

After a while Julie suddenly realized she had been talking a long time. "Gee, I—I'm sorry, Bruce," she said self-consciously. "I don't mean to ramble on like this. It's just that you're such a good listener."

Bruce turned her head around and brought it

to within inches of his. "It's easy when I'm listening to someone so beautiful."

Bruce's warm breath was like a caress. Almost as a reflex, Julie's eyes closed and her mouth opened ever so slightly as she moved closer to Bruce.

Then she felt his arms pushing her gently away from him. "Don't go anywhere, OK?" he said, slowly getting up from the couch.

"Where are you going?" Julie asked, disappointed.

"I have a feeling we're both going to want to remember everything about this moment. I want it all to be perfect. You know, someday we'll think back to what was playing and call it 'our song.' " He winked and flashed her his sexy smile again. "And I know how much you like good music. Let me change the disk to something a little more—special." With that, Bruce walked away, back into the main room.

She nestled back into the couch with a big dreamy smile on her face, feeling as though this were the happiest day of her life.

"I just don't know, Elizabeth," Jessica said. "Maybe you're right."

"Of course I am!" Elizabeth replied. "Come on, you once said those leading roles have the most boring lines. The character people *always* get more applause."

"That's true." Jessica nodded. Her dour mood seemed to have lifted. "Well, I guess I'll *think* about it."

Elizabeth looked around the room. She had been so intent on convincing her twin to take the role that she'd almost forgotten about Julie. She glanced over to the alcove. Bruce and Julie were nowhere to be seen, but that wasn't surprising—it was too dark back there to recognize anybody.

Suddenly she became aware of a new compact disk playing. It was the Summer Wind Consort, a hot new group that played sophisticated jazz-fusion music that was kind of lazy and romantic. She wondered who had had the good taste to put it on.

When she looked over at the CD player, Elizabeth had her answer—Bruce. Her eyes widened as she realized he was with Danielle again. The two of them had obviously just shared some kind of joke because they were both doubled over with laughter. Between spasms of giggles Danielle was giving Bruce playful little kisses.

"Hey, Elizabeth," Jessica called in Elizabeth's ear. "What are you looking at?"

"Oh, sorry! I didn't mean to ignore you. I just got a little distracted."

Jessica looked over in the direction her sister had been staring. "By those two?" she said. "Are you surprised? It makes perfect sense to me that the two snobbiest, most self-centered people in the same room would somehow find each other."

"Remember Lila's rumor, Jessica."

"Oh, that's right—I guess she must have been talking about Danielle! Poor Julie, huh? She's probably home crying or something."

If only that were true, Elizabeth thought. She'd probably be better off than wherever she was right then.

It was as if Bruce had read Julie's mind. She had told him how much she loved classical music, but how could he have known that the Summer Wind Consort was the only pop group she liked? It was proof that she and Bruce belonged together, no matter what anyone else said. As she listened to the music, Julie closed her eyes and thought of Bruce and the feel of his arms around her.

When she opened her eyes, she could see him approaching her in the darkness. In one swift, passionate movement, he swooped down onto the couch and enfolded her in his arms. And as he touched his lips to hers, whatever lingering doubts she had had about him melted away. Julie wanted to hold on to the moment forever, memorize every tiny sensation, every slow, tender movement in their kiss.

And then, without warning, she felt a stinging sensation in her eyes. Some fool had turned the lights on, spoiling the special moment. Julie pulled away, suddenly self-conscious again.

She opened her eyes, shielding them with her hand. What she saw made her body rigid with shock. She was staring right at Josh!

Together they sprang off the couch.

"Josh!" she managed to cry out. "What are *you* doing here?"

"Julie?" he answered. "I—who—this is—"

Julie was completely flabbergasted, and she couldn't stop her next words from babbling out. "You're supposed to be Bruce! I mean, Bruce was . . . What did you do? How dare you?"

Josh waved his arms defensively. "I thought you were . . . Oh, this is unbelievable!"

Slowly a wave of titters began to spread. Everyone in the alcove was staring at them. Near the entrance to the main room a group of people had gathered to see what was going on. Some were laughing out loud, while others covered their mouths to stifle their giggles.

Julie was frozen with shock and embarrassment. Looking around, she realized the whole thing had been a horrible, cruel setup!

Eleven

"What happened back there?" Jessica wondered out loud. She and Elizabeth swung their heads around to follow the commotion.

"I can't tell," Elizabeth answered. She could see that the alcove was now brightly lit, and a group of Phi Epsilon brothers and their dates were looking in. Over by the stereo Bruce and Danielle had erupted into uncontrollable laughter.

All at once the crowd fell silent. Then it moved to the sides to let someone pass—Julie! Elizabeth watched in shock as her friend ran through the room, sobbing. Following close behind, Josh was yelling for her to come back and hear his explanation.

Elizabeth couldn't tell exactly what had happened, but she was willing to bet that Bruce had something to do with it. "We'll talk later, OK, Jess?" she said. "I'm going to see what's up."

Without waiting for her sister to answer, Elizabeth hurried out the front door after Julie. "Julie! Wait for me!" she called out.

Julie was racing down the Patmans' long driveway. She didn't even slow down when Elizabeth shouted her name.

Running as fast as she could, Elizabeth finally caught up to Julie. They both stopped at the trees that separated the grounds of the estate from the street.

Panting, Elizabeth reached out to touch her friend's arm. "Julie, talk to me! What's the matter?"

Julie paced back and forth, fuming. "What's the matter? I'll tell you what's the matter! I'm in a place I don't want to be, with people I never want to see again, and I have absolutely no way of getting home. OK?"

"Julie, please tell me what happened," Elizabeth begged.

But her plea was met with silence. Julie looked as if she were about to explode. Finally she sputtered, "If I ever see any of them again, I'll—I'll *kill* them! How could they do this to me? How could they treat *any* human being like that?"

"*Who*, Julie? Who?"

"Who? Bruce Patman and his whole sadistic, inhuman fraternity. Who else? I'll bet they're all in on this—including my supposed friend Josh!" A single tear ran down Julie's cheek as she spoke. "I should have listened to you Liz. They had this whole thing planned—they *must* have! They all knew I was naive enough to fall for Bruce, that I'd wait on that couch like a stupid puppy dog for him to come back. Ooh, I should have known something was up. I mean, just when we were about to kiss, he went out to change the CD! *Change the CD!* I mean, is that lame or what?"

"Well, what happened when he came back?"

"He didn't—*Josh* did, pretending he was Bruce. And it was too dark to tell the difference. He . . . started kissing me, Liz. I've never let *anyone* do that," she confessed. "It was—it was so wonderful. And there we were, right in the middle of it, when they turned the lights on." She began to shudder. "And when I saw it was Josh, I wanted to die! Oh, Liz, it was horrible. There was a whole roomful of people just standing there, laughing at me!"

Elizabeth was becoming as furious as Julie. "How horrible. This all sounds so vicious!"

"I mean, they might as well have had someone with a bullhorn, taking tickets. It was like, 'Gather round and see her, folks! The world's most incredibly naive girl—humiliated before your own eyes!' How will I ever be able to show my face in school again, Liz!"

As Julie's lips started to quiver and the tears streamed down her cheeks, Elizabeth reached out to her with open arms. "I'm so sorry," she said. "Believe me, I am."

Julie let Elizabeth put her arm around her as she sobbed her heart out. She could only mutter a few choked words, over and over: "I trusted him so much. How could he do this to me?"

"Easy, Julie, easy," Elizabeth said, struggling to find words of comfort. "I know it must be hard. But people will forget this prank, and so will you."

All she could do was hold on to her friend and try to give her as much support as possible. There was no doubt about it now. The "old" Bruce Patman was back—and Julie was his first casualty.

"I don't believe it! Bowen really pulled it off!"

Somehow, despite all the noise in the room, Josh could hear Bruce's voice loud and clear. He felt stunned. The last person he had expected to see on the couch was Julie. He had gone into the alcove expecting another stupid pledge trick—but nothing this horrible!

"Bruce, I can't believe you," Danielle was saying with a guilty little smile. "You're so *bad!*"

"I know," Bruce answered, still red in the face with laughter. "But I just couldn't resist seeing the look on Bowen's face. Hey, way to go, Bowen!" he called out.

Josh was beginning to smolder. He wanted to lash out at Bruce, but an inner voice told him to hold back. *You can patch things up with Julie later*, he said to himself. *But if you blow this chance with Phi Epsilon, you'll never get another one.*

He pulled himself together and walked up to Bruce. He tried to control his temper as he said, "Bruce, I thought I was going to be with someone I didn't know in there."

"Sorry," Bruce said, still smirking. "I didn't know she'd take it so hard. But hey, no reason for *you* to get so uptight about it. It's all part of the pledging. I mean, there are worse-looking girls than Julie!"

Ronnie Edwards, Tom McKay, and a couple of other brothers and pledges were listening to the conversation. Around them, people had begun dancing and talking again. "What was the point, Bruce?" Josh asked. He had to fight against sounding hostile. "I'm just wondering. I mean, is it true all the pledges were going to go back there, just like I did?"

Bruce laughed. In a loud voice so everyone around him could hear, he said, "Sure, Bowen! Like I told you before, it was a *contest*, for the best lover among the pledges. Looks like you really bombed out, judging from the girl's reaction."

A couple of other brothers laughed along with Bruce, although most of the group seemed turned off by the whole thing. Winston Egbert, for one, walked away shaking his head.

"Yeah," Josh continued, "and you also said you'd gotten a girl who no one really knew to be the judge of the contest—but you knew that I was friends with Julie!"

"OK, OK, I'll admit it," Bruce answered smugly. "I just wanted to do an experiment— isn't that right, boys?"

Ronnie nodded. "A physics experiment, I believe," he said.

"Precisely, Professor Edwards," Bruce replied. He put on a mock serious tone. "Question: Can two bodies of the human species who have no visible attraction to each other nevertheless be induced to kiss passionately? Answer: Yes, under the proper circumstances and with proper lighting! Class dismissed!"

Bruce's friends laughed again, and Josh caught a glimpse of Danielle, eyeing Bruce with admiration. The whole scene sickened him. For a brief moment he considered hauling off and punching Bruce. But instead, he just turned his back and walked away.

"Gee, I guess I must have touched a sensitive nerve," Bruce said, pretending to be concerned. "They just don't make pledges like they used to."

Josh didn't know what to do next. As a pledge he had to stay at the party and clean up after it was over. He was too embarrassed to call Julie and too depressed to have a good time. Maybe food would work. His shoulders slumping forward, he went into the adjoining room, where the food had been set out.

"Hey, want some hors d'oeuvres?" a voice asked. Josh looked around and saw Winston Egbert sitting on a chair in corner of the room, holding a bag of potato chips in one hand and dipping a chip in a bowl of onion dip on a table with the other.

"Sure," Josh answered. He walked over and grabbed a handful from the bag Winston held out to him.

Together they munched on the chips, concentrating on getting as much dip as possible onto each chip. Finally Winston said, "Delicious. And when we polish this off, there's some clam dip left. I swear, this stuff is going to save the party for me."

"Imagine that," Josh said with a wry smile. "Someone else besides me is having a miserable time."

"Well, my girlfriend, Maria, couldn't come because she had to visit her aunt in San Diego. But to tell you the truth, it was that scene with you and Julie that really got me down. I don't know, Josh. I'm into the fraternity as much as the next guy—when it's in good fun. But this year the pledging's really gotten out of hand. Especially with certain guys who shall remain nameless—like Bruce." Suddenly he looked left and right with a mischievous smile and covered his mouth with his hand. "Don't you ever tell anyone I said that!"

"No, no, I won't."

Winston sighed. "To be honest with you, Josh, I don't see why you still want to join Phi Epsilon. I mean, we're not as bad as you probably think we are—it's just that Bruce's faction has gotten so powerful this year. It wasn't like this last year."

"Faction?"

"Yeah, it's like there are two different groups. The good guys"—Winston smiled—"like yours truly, and the others, Bruce and his gang. For a while there it seemed like Bruce had changed. But lately he's been up to his old tricks. I think he wants to get as many of his friends into Phi Epsilon as he can."

"That figures," Josh said, taking a huge potato chip out of the half-empty bag. "You know, it's too bad. My brother always told me what a great group Phi Epsilon was. He said it was the only thing that made him want to go to school."

"Ah-h-h, yes," said Winston in an old man's voice. "I remember the old days. Things'll never be the same. . . ."

But Josh was too wrapped up in his thoughts to notice Winston's imitation. "In a funny way," he said, "it makes me want to be in even more. I want to help bring Phi Epsilon back to the way it was."

"Well, I certainly wouldn't get in your way. If you think you could actually enjoy being in a group with Bruce. . . ." Winston chuckled. "It might be more trouble than it's worth."

The back room had an entire kitchen set-up, and Josh opened the refrigerator to get out a bottle of soda. He thought about Winston's statement. It seemed strange that an actual member of Phi Epsilon would be so negative about the fraternity—or about certain brothers, anyway.

Just then, out of the corner of his eye, Josh saw Elizabeth walking across the dance floor in the main room. There was a serious look on her face as she approached Jeffrey. The two of them talked intently for a minute, and Jeffrey reached into his pocket to give her a set of keys. Then Elizabeth walked out.

Josh had a feeling that Elizabeth was probably about to drive Julie home in Jeffrey's car. She must have caught up to Julie outside. His mind ran through the nightmarish events of the evening. He could see the pain on Julie's face, and he knew it would be hard for them to be friends again. *I've got to say something to her*, he decided. "Have some soda, Winston," he said, offering the other boy a bottle of Coke. "It goes well with all that salt. I've got to run. See you later!"

Josh darted through the party room, up the stairs, and out the front door. Guided by the pale white glow of the gravel in the moonlight, he ran down the driveway. In the distance he thought he could hear someone crying softly. "Elizabeth? Julie?" he called out. But as he got to the street, all he heard was the roar of a car pulling away.

Josh stood on the street, listening to his own panting in the cool night air. The thought of what he had done in that alcove suddenly struck him like a sledgehammer. He could barely remember not knowing Julie, not having her as a friend—and now she would probably never speak to him again. *And I brought it all on myself by wanting to be in Phi Ep so badly*, he realized.

Just then Winston's words came back to Josh: "It might be more trouble than it's worth." Josh wondered if Winston might be right.

Twelve

"I don't know, Liz," Julie said outside math class the next Monday. "I'm not really up for duets after school today. I think I'll just go straight home. I'm feeling pretty tired."

"That's all right." Elizabeth smiled, then looked at Julie, clearly concerned about her. "You're still upset about Friday, aren't you?"

"No, I think I'm over that. Thanks for driving me home afterward, though. Our talk really helped."

"So when do you want me to slip the arsenic into Bruce's milk shake—tomorrow at lunch?"

Julie managed a half-smile. "I'd rather see him get sick on ice-cream sundaes, just like Josh."

Josh. It made Julie cringe just to say his name. The whole weekend she had rocketed back and forth from anger to disbelief to humiliation. Bruce's cruel trick was bad enough, but somehow Josh's betrayal had been even harder to take.

"Well, I'll see what I can do," Elizabeth replied, shifting her books from one arm to the other. "Hmm. I wonder if we can get him to pledge Phi Beta Alpha."

The image of Bruce pledging the sorority would have been funny to Julie if she weren't so repulsed by the very thought of him.

"Listen, take care of yourself," Elizabeth said, "and whenever you want to practice, just holler." She grinned and imitated playing a recorder. "Or squeak!"

Julie watched Elizabeth disappear down the hallway. She contemplated calling out to her and telling her the truth—that she *hadn't* gotten over the party, that she thought she wouldn't even if she lived to be a hundred. But she couldn't bring herself to burden her new friend again, not after all the time Elizabeth had spent consoling her on Friday.

Julie's number-one goal was to go through the day without having to see anyone from the party. She kept her head down as she rounded the hallway toward her next class.

But right in the hallway between Julie and

the classroom was a large crowd of students. They were gathered around, watching something, and most of them were laughing. Terribly-played accordion music was echoing in the hall. Julie quickly walked alongside the wall, hoping no one would notice her.

As she passed the crowd she saw two boys in the middle, both with their backs toward her. One was standing up and playing the accordion, and the other was on a long leash, dancing around like a monkey. Girls in the crowd were giggling hysterically as the boy leapt up from his monkeylike crouch and kissed them on the cheek.

Another stupid pledge assignment, Julie thought. *I can't seem to get away from them.* The boy started jumping around the edge of the crowd nearest Julie. She couldn't see his face, but he was spinning wildly, kissing every girl in sight. Julie stepped up her pace.

Just as she passed by, without any warning, the boy whirled around and planted a loud kiss on her lips.

"Oh!" she couldn't help but cry out in dismay. The crowd let out a big laugh, and Julie wanted to run away. Then she saw who had kissed her.

It was Josh, *again!* Julie felt paralyzed by her humiliation. She wanted to run, to scream, to hit him, to cry—but all of those impulses just seemed to cancel each other out, and all she could do was stand still and stare at him.

The boy with the accordion turned around, and Julie saw Ronnie Edwards's face. Suddenly he stopped playing and muttered, "Uh-oh."

"Julie!" Josh exclaimed. "Uh, sorry, I didn't know . . ."

Julie opened her mouth to yell at him, but nothing came out.

"I can explain everything!" Josh said.

Jerking away from him, Julie backed against the wall. Her jaw was so tight that when she spoke, the words came out through clenched teeth. "Fine, Josh, explain everything," she taunted. "Give everyone something else to laugh about. Tell them *all* what you did to me—in graphic detail! Only do me one small favor, if you can. Just wait until I'm out of sight!" With that, she turned to run away.

"No, wait!" Josh cried out, grabbing her arm. Julie's books flew onto the floor, making a loud, clattering noise.

"Leave me alone!" Julie screamed. She grabbed her books off the floor and bolted down the hallway, trying to put as much distance as possible between her and Josh—and the laughing crowd of people who seemed to surround them wherever they were.

* * *

Don't take it so seriously. There are a bunch of us rooting for you. Josh repeated John Pfeifer's words to himself over and over again as he walked outside after class. He'd had a whole weekend to think about whether he wanted to stick it out with Phi Epsilon. At first there was no question—he was determined to quit, to tell Bruce exactly what he thought of him. But each time he made up his mind, a nagging question haunted him: would he be better off quitting, or worse? As it was, Julie would probably never talk to him again, whether he quit or not. And quitting would only alienate everyone in the fraternity, including the guys he liked. Not to mention the fact that Phil would be completely disappointed in him.

There seemed to be no choice. He'd gone too far to back out now. All he could do was stick out the last week—and hope he didn't run into Bruce too often.

As if on cue, a loud voice interrupted his thoughts. "There you are, Bowen!" Josh felt himself cringe involuntarily as he turned to see Bruce and Ronnie approaching. It was as if Bruce had a homing device to find him.

"Hey, Bruce," he said dryly, trying to keep from sounding disgusted at the sight of him.

Bruce threw his arm around Josh. "Well, this is your final week as a pledge, Josh, and you know something? We've all come to the conclusion that you have really paid your dues."

Ronnie nodded in agreement as the three of them strolled across Sweet Valley High's rolling lawn.

"You were both a sexy blond receptionist *and* a killer Don Juan at the party, and Ronnie here tells me you were an excellent monkey this afternoon."

Excellent—yeah right, Josh thought. *I ended up hurting Julie all over again because of that stupid act.*

The three boys stopped in front of a white oak tree right by the sidewalk. "What brother Bruce is trying to say," Ronnie added, "is that we've decided to take it easy on you for your last few days."

Josh couldn't believe it. They were actually going to let him go home right after school for a change. He smiled. "Thanks, guys—"

"So we'll only make you do *fifty* push-ups before you go home today," Bruce interrupted, grinning.

Josh glanced around him. Students were pouring out of the building. They would all walk right by and see him involved in yet another pledge ritual. *Why are all these things so public?* Josh thought. *Everyone in the school has seen me in some kind of humiliating situation. They must all think I'm a real wimp.*

Reluctantly Josh got on his hands and knees.

"One!" Bruce called out. "Two! Three!"

Josh had been through this before. Bruce would "lose count" at twenty-nine or so and go back to twenty. And before Josh knew it, his arms would feel as if they were going to fall off. The worst thing about it was the stares of the people who passed by—cold and uncaring, recognizing how childish the whole thing was.

As Josh made it to his fortieth push-up, he thought he heard snickering from someone going by.

"Forty-three. Come on, Bowen!" Bruce bellowed for everyone to hear. "Every Phi Ep can do at least a hundred of these! Forty-four . . ."

Josh grunted and his arms began to shake violently. He wanted to show Bruce he could do it, make it all the way to fifty, so he pushed . . . pushed—and collapsed to the ground at forty-five.

"O-h-h-h, what a shame," Bruce said. "It's too bad, Bowen. I was planning a surprise for you—no more pledge assignments for the rest of the week if you'd finished all fifty."

Ronnie sighed and shrugged his shoulders. "I guess that means he'll just have to keep it up until he gets it right."

"But take heart, Bowen. We'll only tack on five bonus push-ups for tomorrow. Come along, Ronald. And don't forget to rest up, pledge. That means *no* helping your mother with the vacuuming this week, no matter how much you like it!''

As the two boys walked away, laughing hysterically, Josh sat against the tree and caught his breath. He let himself relax for a few minutes and watched the last group of students straggling out of the school, including Elizabeth.

Josh felt himself freeze up inside. He wanted to ask her about Julie, but he knew Elizabeth probably hated him now. He could just imagine all the bitter things Julie had said about him after the party.

He turned away and started walking. *This is so frustrating*, he said to himself, kicking a pebble along the ground. *No one knows my side of the story—except the Phi Epsilon guys.* The whole thing seemed hopeless, until he heard Elizabeth's voice behind him.

"Hey, Josh! Hold on!"

Josh turned around and pretended to be surprised. "Oh, hi, Elizabeth," he said, scuffing the toe of his shoe on the ground.

"Are you taking the bus?" she asked. "I have to go to the dentist."

Well, at least she wasn't tearing him apart yet, Josh thought. Maybe he could explain the situation to Elizabeth and she could get through to Julie.

"No, I've got my car. I'll be glad to drop you off at your dentist's, though."

"Thanks," Elizabeth said, "I can't seem to get our car away from Jessica lately."

As they walked toward the parking lot, Josh said, "Listen, Elizabeth, I want to talk to you about the frat party."

Elizabeth laughed. "Well, I'm glad you brought it up. I was expecting both of us to beat around the bush a little longer."

Josh felt a huge weight lift from his shoulders. "You have no idea what a relief it is to be able to talk about this. The truth is, I had no idea that was Julie back in that room. It was a setup. . . ."

Josh described the whole story as they drove. Elizabeth listened intently, the look on her face growing more and more serious. When Josh finished, he asked if she would tell Julie what he said.

Elizabeth fell silent for a moment.

"Well, don't you believe me?" Josh asked.

"Yes, I believe you, Josh," Elizabeth said. "But I really think you should be the one to tell her."

Josh pounded the wheel of the car in frustration. "I've tried, Liz. She wouldn't take my phone calls all weekend, and whenever I went to her house, her dad said she wasn't home. And I won't even tell you what a disaster today has been." He glanced at Elizabeth pleadingly. "I-I know we barely know each other, and

137

you must think I'm a total jerk, but . . . well, Julie really means a lot to me, and I'd hate to lose her as a friend." He didn't want to admit how deeply he'd *really* started to feel about Julie. It was hard enough to admit that to himself.

Elizabeth sighed. "Well, I guess I could try, Josh. But to tell you the truth, I don't know if she'll listen." She hesitated a moment, then said, "Do you mind if I ask you a question?"

"No," he replied with a shrug.

"Do you really think this pledging thing is worth all the trouble?"

"I don't know, Liz," Josh said, staring intently at the road ahead. "I've been so mixed up about all of this lately. I mean, Phi Epsilon's always been a good fraternity. I remember how proud my brother was to be in it. And I really like some of the guys in it, like Winston, John, Bill Chase . . ."

"I notice you haven't mentioned the name Bruce Patman," Elizabeth added.

"Oh, don't get me started. I don't know if I can ever forgive him for what he did to Julie."

Elizabeth smiled gently. "Well, maybe your relationship with Julie deserves more attention than Phi Epsilon, Josh."

Josh nodded, until he glanced over at Elizabeth and saw the meaningful stare she was giving him. "Oh"—he chuckled—"well, I don't think of Julie *that* way. I mean, we're friends, but not—you know . . ."

By this time they had reached downtown Sweet Valley. "This is where I get out, Josh," Elizabeth said. "Thanks for the ride. I'll tell Julie what you said."

Josh pulled the car over to the curb and stopped. "Thanks, Elizabeth. I really appreciate it. See you tomorrow!"

After Elizabeth got out, John continued slowly up the street, thinking about Julie and about what Elizabeth had said to him. *My relationship with Julie*, he thought. It sounded good. It sounded *right*. The more Josh thought about it, the more he realized how strong his feelings for Julie were. And it must be starting to show, Josh realized, if Elizabeth could pick up on it. For the first time since Friday, Josh felt himself smiling.

Thirteen

Elizabeth sat quietly in the auditorium. It was only Tuesday, the second day of rehearsals, but already Jessica had been having a crisis. The night before, she had come home upset that the first rehearsal had been a disaster. Mr. Jaworski had been picking on her, she said. Elizabeth figured she'd offer to sit in on a rehearsal and give her notes, and to her surprise, Jessica had agreed.

With a critical eye Elizabeth watched her twin as she began leaping in the air, her feet beating together exactly the way Madame André had taught the entrechat all those years ago.

"OK, stop! Stop!" Mr. Jaworski called out in a weary voice. He put down his clipboard and walked up to the stage. "Look, I don't want to belabor this scene. It shouldn't be taking us the whole rehearsal. Neil, you and Richard are fine. Jessica, it's still not there! What happened to the spirit I saw in your audition? These movements are supposed to be *funny*, remember?"

He climbed onto the stage and stood beside Jessica. "This is a sight gag. While those two are talking, they both forget all about you." He began jumping up and down wildly, looking completely uncoordinated. "And you're leaping around like a jack-in-the-box. If you're too *good* at it, the audience won't laugh."

Everyone on stage broke into laughter at Mr. Jaworski's movements, and Elizabeth had to giggle, too. But she couldn't help noticing the frown on her twin's face.

They ran the scene over again. This time Jessica's entrechats looked a little more awkward, and the scene went fairly well.

"Not bad," Mr. Jaworski called out. "Jessica, you're on the right track. I still want to see more, though." He looked at his watch and clapped his hands briskly. "All right, kids, let's take five. We'll come back with Ed's first entrance."

Jessica stalked off the stage and into the aisle. She shot a quick glance at Elizabeth, but she didn't break her stride as she walked toward the exit.

Elizabeth followed her sister into the hallway, where Jessica let out a little scream of frustration. "I can't do it!"

"That last time was a big improvement," Elizabeth said. "Just keep trying, Jess. All you have to do is loosen up a little."

"Now you sound like Mr. Jaworski! What am I supposed to do, move like a football player? Next thing you know, he'll have me putting on shoulder pads!"

"Jessica, you're going a little overboard. This is a comedy. I think some of the lines are hilarious, and I can see what Mr. Jaworski is saying. You *knew* you were going to have to dance badly. It's part of the character! What about all those crazy things you did at the audition?"

Jessica frowned. She leaned up against the wall and looked down at her feet. "That was different. I exaggerated because I thought Mr. Jaworski wanted me to, for a character exercise." She looked up into Elizabeth's eyes. "But don't you see? This is for real! I can't do that in a performance. People will think I'm a total klutz. I thought I could just dance a *little* wrong— you know, just enough to let everyone know I really knew what I was doing. I mean, my acting can take care of the rest."

"Nobody's saying you can't act, Jessica. But if you try to look too pretty, and too coordinated, then no one will pay attention to you. That's

not the way the part is supposed to be played."
Jessica started to protest, but Elizabeth cut her
off. "Look," she continued, "you wanted me to
come and give you my opinion, right? Now, *I*
know you can do it, but I have to be honest. If
you can't really get into it, back out and let
someone else do the part."

Jessica looked as if she had been mortally
wounded. "That's easy for you to say. I'd like
to see how *you'd* feel if you were up there!"

"Oh, come on, Jess, you know what I mean—"

But Jessica wasn't going to listen to any more
criticism. She stormed back into the auditorium.

Elizabeth started to follow her sister, but just
then she heard a familiar sound. She listened
closely. She could make out the strains of a
haunting recorder melody, wafting through the
hallway on the side of the auditorium.

She turned away from the auditorium and
walked toward the practice rooms. As she got
closer she was struck by the hollow sadness of
the tune. She remembered what Julie had said
that day about the piano: "My playing always
seems to match my mood."

Elizabeth sighed. *I guess I should see how she's
doing.*

With the door to the practice room closed,
Julie felt isolated from the world—exactly the

way she wanted to be. As she played the recorder, she could feel herself calming down and the pain of the last few days disappearing. There was no need to see anybody, talk to anybody, have any human contact at all . . .

And when there was a sudden knock at the door, she didn't even want to see who it was.

"Julie? It's me, Elizabeth."

Julie heard the muffled voice through the thick wooden door, but she pretended she hadn't. The last thing she wanted to do was practice with Elizabeth. If she did, she'd have to pretend she was in a good mood. And she knew Elizabeth would ask her all kinds of questions about Josh, and then the monkey incident would come up, and Julie would have to feel stupid and embarrassed all over again.

There was another knock, and Julie continued to play as if she were too swept up in the music to hear anything else. Julie felt a little guilty about ignoring her friend, but she desperately wanted to be left alone. She reached over to her music stand for another piece of music.

The practice room door slowly opened. "Safe to come in?" Elizabeth asked.

Julie spun around in her chair and tried to act surprised. "Oh, hi, Elizabeth. I was just, uh, fooling around. Actually, I'm about to go home."

She stood up to reach for her instrument case,

but Elizabeth walked in and sat down. "That was an incredibly sad song."

"I guess it was," Julie agreed, putting away her recorder. She turned toward the door, trying to look as composed as possible. "Well, I'll see you tomorrow. Maybe we can practice after school." She opened the door and stepped through.

"I spoke to Josh yesterday," Elizabeth said matter-of-factly.

Julie stopped in her tracks. She had vowed never to have anything to do with Josh again—not see him, not even speak about him. But somehow, when Elizabeth mentioned his name, Julie wanted to stay. She wanted to hear what he'd said.

"He asked me all about you," Elizabeth continued.

"Yeah?"

"But . . . well, I guess it can wait. I know you're in a hurry, and I wouldn't want to keep you."

"No," Julie replied, stepping back in and gently closing the door behind her. "No, that's all right. What did he say?"

"Well, he told me his version of what happened at the party."

"Oh, really?" Julie laughed sarcastically. "Did he find it as funny as everyone else seemed to?"

"Not exactly. In fact, he said he had no idea that it was you on the couch."

"I see. He makes it a habit of going into dark alcoves and kissing strange girls."

"No, Julie. It wasn't like that. He was told it was some kind of contest, supposedly for best kisser among the pledges. He was set up by Bruce—"

"Oh, *that's* great to hear! And I was the guinea pig, right? *All* the pledges were going to come my way—Josh was just breaking me in?" It was even worse than Julie had imagined.

"But Josh—"

"Oooh! Those—those animals! If that isn't the lowest, dirtiest, most *inhuman*—"

"Julie, you're right to be mad, but it's *Bruce* you should be mad at, not Josh!" Elizabeth argued. "He feels terrible about it, and he's furious at Bruce!"

It took all Julie's strength to keep from screaming. "Tell me one thing, Elizabeth. Did he say that he was going to back out of pledging?"

"Well, no, but—"

"Of course not! That stupid fraternity is the most important thing in the world to him—much more important than I am! For weeks he's done anything Bruce has told him to do, no matter how embarrassing! How do you expect me to believe he didn't know about this? For all I know, he told Bruce he *enjoyed* it!" Once again tears clouded Julie's eyes.

146

"Julie, all I can tell you is what I heard. I really believe that Josh cares about you, a lot more than you know."

Julie tried to seem disinterested. "Mm-hmm. Well, thanks for telling me, Elizabeth. You've been a really good friend to me throughout this whole mess. But I think I'd like to be alone for a while, if you don't mind."

Elizabeth nodded and stood up. "Sure, Julie. Just remember, you can always call me if you want to talk."

"OK, I will," Julie replied, forcing a smile. "See you later."

Julie waited a few moments after Elizabeth left, and then, for what felt like the millionth time, she gave in to a tidal wave of tears. But this time it felt a little different. It was something deeper than anger or embarrassment, and she wasn't thinking about Bruce at all. She knew she was crying because of some strange, strong feelings for Josh—some feelings that she didn't quite understand yet.

Fourteen

Oh, no, Josh thought as he stood in the cafeteria line. *Another relaxing lunch, ruined by Bruce Patman.* He turned away, hoping Bruce wouldn't see him for once.

Bruce strolled past Josh to the head of the line. "Come on, Edwards! You're not doing hot lunch, are you?"

"Hey," Ronnie replied from somewhere in front of Josh. "Some of our parents have to work for a living. They can't afford live-in butlers and maids who make their lunch every day!"

Bruce laughed. "All right, stuff your face with that swill. I'll go check and see if anyone has a stomach pump."

Glancing over his shoulder, Josh saw Bruce saunter over to a table full of Phi Epsilon brothers. It seemed to Josh as if they were all sitting there today—Winston, Bill, Tom, Allen, and John—all except him.

Josh scanned the cafeteria quickly. He hadn't seen Elizabeth or Julie all day, and he really wanted to know whether or not they'd gotten a chance to talk about what had happened at the party. He surveyed the room until he found Elizabeth. He had to get through the lunch line and walk to Elizabeth's table without being seen by the Phi Epsilon guys. It was going to be hard, but Josh was determined. He had already heard from one of the other pledges that something was brewing. Apparently the fraternity had cooked up some new, outrageous antics to pack into the three remaining pledge days—today, Thursday, and Friday.

When Ronnie paid for his food and headed over to the fraternity table, tray in hand, Josh adjusted his Angels baseball cap so that it covered his forehead and slipped into the serving area. He zipped through, picking up some beef stroganoff and a salad. Then he carefully kept his back to the Phi Epsilon guys as he walked over to Elizabeth's table on the opposite end of the cafeteria.

Elizabeth was facing the wall, writing on a yellow pad. "Don't say my name, and let me sit next to you instead of across from you, OK?" Josh said into her ear as he sat down.

Elizabeth looked around with a start. "Sure, Josh. What's going on? Is Bruce making you pretend to be James Bond today?"

"Bruce isn't making me do anything—at least not yet. Look, I'm sure I don't have much time before he figures out where I am, so tell me everything."

"Everything about what?"

"You know, about what Julie said when you told her why I kissed her!"

Elizabeth laughed. "Just out of curiosity, right? I mean, it's not like you really *care* for her or anything. . . ."

Josh smiled. He wouldn't dare admit it to Elizabeth, but since their conversation, he had been thinking a lot about Julie. And he had finally admitted the truth to himself—that he cared for Julie more than he ever had for any girl. Ever since he was small he had thought of Julie as just a friend—the girl next door who played piano and walked to school with him. It had been that way for so long that it was hard to see the changes that had happened right under his nose.

"Just tell me, OK?" he pleaded. "I don't know how much longer I have." He cautiously glanced around him and caught a glimpse of Bruce giving orders to a few pledges.

"Well, I hate to tell you this, but Julie is really upset. She still thinks you were in on the whole thing. She's convinced that if you weren't, you would have been upset enough to quit Phi Epsilon after what happened at the party."

"But she doesn't understand—"

"I'm just telling you what she said," Elizabeth interrupted.

"Excuse me, sir . . . madam," a squeaky voice came from above them. "Would you like to order a beverage? Perhaps something from our fine collection of Sweet Valley vintages?"

Both Josh and Elizabeth looked over their shoulders to see one of the pledges, Andy Snyder, holding cartons of chocolate milk in his hands. "Oh, hi, Josh," Andy said.

"Andy," Josh said in a tense whisper, "don't you *dare* tell Bruce I'm here, or I'll—"

"Hey, no problem," Andy said with a look of envy. "I'll just move on."

Next to them Josh heard a voice say, "May I take your plate, ma'am?" Behind them another voice said, "Is everything all right here? Can I get you anything?"

All around the cafeteria Josh could see pledges waiting on tables, clearing trays, and seating bewildered students who had just emerged from the lunch line. A wave of laughter rolled through the cafeteria, and even the kitchen staffers came out to see what was going on.

"See what you're missing, Josh?" Elizabeth said with a raised eyebrow.

"Elizabeth, you have to talk to Julie again. Tell her—"

Before he could finish his sentence, Josh felt a strong grip on his shoulder. He looked up to see Bruce leering at him. "Well, it looks like one of our waiters has decided to skip a shift," he said.

Josh felt trapped. He had to figure out a way to get Julie to forgive him, and Elizabeth was his only hope. "Hey, Bruce! How's it going?" he asked politely. "Uh, look, could you give me a couple more minutes? I have to ask Elizabeth something—"

"Well, will you listen to this! Here we are, short-staffed, with hundreds of customers waiting for service, and *you* want a couple more minutes! Forget it, Bowen. Get to work!" Bruce winked at Elizabeth. "Excuse us."

"Come on, Bruce," Josh protested. "This is really important."

"Hey, if you think it's unfair, take it up with the union boss!"

Bruce was glaring down at Josh. And Elizabeth was looking on expectantly, as if she were waiting for Josh to defy Bruce. For a moment Josh thought he would stay put. But another thought popped into his mind: *Let's see exactly what he wants me to do. If it's really awful, I can always tell him to get lost.*

Shrugging his shoulders, Josh stood up from the table. Elizabeth looked a little disappointed, and Josh wondered if he had made the wrong decision. "I'll see you later, OK?" he said, trying not to sound too anxious. "Maybe we can talk after school."

"Maybe," Elizabeth agreed. She went back to writing.

Josh followed Bruce to the table where the Phi Epsilon guys were sitting. Bruce remained standing and gestured for Josh to take his seat. "Gentleman," Bruce announced in a phony, pompous voice, "I have captured the missing employee in his hiding place—by the side of another one of his girlfriends, of course. Now, what shall we give him as a punishment?"

John said, "Come on, Bruce, give the guy a break."

"Nonsense!" Bruce replied. "Let the punishment fit the crime. Hmm, maybe I'll have him kiss the cashiers. . . ."

"Just let him clear some tables or something," Winston suggested.

Bruce's eyes wandered about the room. Suddenly they focused on something and his face lit up. "No, *I* know exactly what soon-to-be-brother Bowen shall do to repent."

Josh followed Bruce's gaze. The cafeteria was

getting pretty full by now. Some of Elizabeth's friends had joined her at one table, Jessica and Lila were chatting at another but finally Josh saw who Bruce was staring at: Julie. She was just about to sit down by herself at a table near the exit. *No*, Josh thought with dread. *He's not going to involve her again.*

The corners of Bruce's mouth curled up in a devilish grin as he leaned closer to Josh's face. "Your girlfriend looks awfully lonely over there, doesn't she?"

Josh looked into Bruce's eyes, hoping to see a sign that he was joking.

"I think you ought to bring her a treat, Bowen." He grabbed Ronnie's plastic plate and, using a napkin, wiped off whatever Ronnie hadn't eaten. Then he pulled three one-dollar bills out of his pocket. "No use wasting the fine china," he said, handing Josh the plate with the money on it.

Josh took the plate tentatively. Was Bruce going to make him try to buy back Julie's affection? The idea made him sick.

"That money ought to buy you, oh, about six bowls of Jell-O, right? That should make a lovely, delicious dessert. You can arrange it all in a creative way on this plate and then serve it graciously to your, ah, *special friend*," Bruce explained.

Josh couldn't believe this. If he went through

with this prank, there was no way that Julie would ever speak to him again—not to mention the fact that she would be humiliated in public for the third time in less than a week. He couldn't do that to her.

For what seemed like hours, Josh stood still, staring blankly at the plate. Every pair of eyes at the table was trained on him. He couldn't decide what to do. The voices around him sounded muffled, as if they were underwater.

"Well, come *on*, Bowen," Bruce said. "Old Julie will think nobody loves her!"

That did it. Josh could put up with Bruce insulting *him*, but not Julie. She didn't deserve that. Josh put the plate back down on the table. "No, Bruce," he said firmly. "I won't."

"What?" Bruce said, glowering menacingly. "Tell me I heard wrong. Tell me you said, 'Yes, Bruce, right away.' "

Josh shook his head. "No, I won't do this."

"Well, well, a rebel without a cause. Or should I say, a rebel without a fraternity? Because if you *don't* do this, Bowen, it's weeks down the drain, and no Phi Epsilon. I don't care whether your brother was a member or not."

Josh was beginning to feel weak inside. *Phil wouldn't understand why I got kicked out*, he thought. *He'd think I was just too wimpy to survive the pledging*.

"Do it, Bowen, or you're out. I'm giving you

three seconds to decide. Consider yourself lucky to have that long. One . . ."

Thoughts were tumbling through Josh's brain. If he could just have some more time to figure it all out . . .

"Two . . ."

Suddenly everything became crystal clear to Josh. He knew what he had to do.

"Three!"

Josh grabbed the plate off the table and strode toward the serving line.

"That's it, Bowen!" Bruce shouted. "Now, don't forget—get all different colors!"

This late in the lunch period there weren't very many people in line, and Josh found an empty spot in front of the desserts. He took six bowls of all the different flavored Jell-O—cherry, lime, orange, lemon, and two with mixed fruit in them. He dumped all the bowls onto the plate, making a huge mountain of gelatin.

"Hey!" the cashier called out. "What do you think you're doing?"

"Don't worry," Josh said with a reassuring smile. "I'm paying for it all." He showed her the six empty bowls, gave her the three dollars, and picked up the plate. "Just love that Jell-O!" he added cheerily.

The heaping, multicolored mass jiggled crazily as Josh stepped back into the eating area, and a roar of laughter erupted from the Phi

Epsilon table. Then, curious about the sudden noise, other people in the cafeteria turned to look at Josh.

Before long just above everyone there was staring at him—Jessica, Lila, Elizabeth . . . and Julie. When Josh's eyes darted over to Julie's corner, she immediately looked down—but not soon enough for Josh to miss the hurt and confusion in her eyes.

Josh walked slowly toward her with the plate. The Jell-O moved as if it were alive. Whoops and cheers rang out from the fraternity table.

"What a guy!" Bruce yelled out, red in the face with laughter. "She'll love you for this, Bowen!"

But when Josh was halfway there, he stopped. Then, without warning, he took a sharp right and picked up his pace, heading right for the fraternity table.

With a mushy-sounding splat, Josh dumped the entire plate of Jell-O right into Bruce Patman's lap.

Bruce shot up from his seat in shock, sending Jell-O flying in all directions. "Aaaaah! My new pants!"

There was a moment of silence, and then a ripple of laughter swept through the room. A handful of people even applauded.

Two Phi Epsilon brothers jumped up and held

onto Josh's arms tightly, so that he couldn't run away.

"Forget him!" Bruce said, wiping the Jell-O off his pants. Then he looked at Josh, his face bright red. "You'll pay for this, Bowen!" he snarled. "This is the stupidest thing you've ever done."

Josh felt as if he were seeing Bruce for the first time. Standing with a stained pair of pants, a pile of brightly colored Jell-O at his feet, he looked powerless and pathetic. "Why is that, Bruce?" he asked. "Because you'll block me from getting into Phi Epsilon?"

"Well, you're not as dumb as you look," Bruce shot back. "You'd better believe I'll block you! You're *history* as far as Phi Ep is concerned."

"Good," Josh said with a grin. "Because that saves me the trouble of telling you that I quit! You can try your stupid tricks on someone else, Bruce, because I'm not your pledge anymore."

"Yahoo!" a voice called out from behind him. Josh couldn't tell who it was, but he could hear laughter all around him now. He turned away from Bruce. To his left he could see Lila and Jessica giggling. Over by the wall Elizabeth was standing up and applauding. And Josh could feel his own face light up as he saw Julie, sitting near the exit, laughing.

Now there was only one thing on his mind. He made his way through the aisles of the

158

cafeteria toward Julie's table. She was staring at him, not with the hatred he had seen after the monkey incident but with what looked like a mixture of fear and hope.

A minute ago Josh would have been scared, too, but right now he felt stronger than he had felt in his entire life. "I have to talk to you," he announced to Julie. "Privately."

Julie looked down at the floor, and for a moment Josh thought she was going to say no. Then she looked up at him with sad eyes and said, "OK, Josh."

Josh led Julie out of the cafeteria, and they found a quiet corner in the hallway.

Josh faced Julie, then looked away, trying to find the words he wanted to say. Suddenly, out of the corner of his eye, he saw Bruce, angrily stomping out of the cafeteria and heading for the men's room. On his heels were two other Phi Epsilon members.

"I can't believe this!" Bruce was saying. "You know how much work the tailor did on these?"

"Hey, it's OK," one of the others answered. "My mom gets stains out by using club soda."

"Talcum powder," the other one suggested.

"I'm so glad I've got the Sweet Valley Homemakers Club with me," Bruce grumbled as they all pushed their way through the bathroom door.

Josh could feel a big smile growing on his face. But he had wanted a quiet, serious mo ment with Julie, so he tried to keep back the smile. He looked at her and was met by a pair of twinkling eyes.

Together, as if on cue, both of them burst out laughing. Josh was seized with the urge to wrap his arms around Julie, to comfort her and tell her that he had quit the fraternity because of her. But he felt as if he should take things more slowly. It would probably take a long time for Julie to get over her hurt.

"I wanted to apologize . . ." Josh began.

Julie smiled at him and nodded. "I know," she said. "But you don't have to. Elizabeth told me what really happened at the party."

"And you believe it?"

Julie put her hands on her hips. "Well, shouldn't I? Was she telling a lie?"

"Yes! I mean, no! I mean—"

"It's OK, Josh," Julie said with a warm smile. "It *was* hard for me to believe Elizabeth. I thought I'd never forgive you for humiliating me."

"But, Julie, it wasn't me—"

"I see that now, Josh. I guess I was looking for a sign. A sign that you"—she looked down and began to blush—"cared enough about me to quit the fraternity. Oooh, I don't believe I'm telling you this. I mean, I know I have no right to expect—"

"Yes, you do!" Josh interrupted. "I *do* care about you, Julie."

Julie's face was radiant. "Well, I definitely got my sign, right there in the cafeteria."

Josh nodded. Suddenly he felt a little embarrassed, but there was something he had to tell Julie. "I guess we're both looking for signs."

Josh looked into Julie's joyful eyes. And before he knew it, he felt her arms wrapping around him and her warm lips pressing his. "How's that?" she said.

"Mmm. Second best kiss I've ever had."

Julie tore herself away from him. "Second? Who was the first?"

"Some girl I met at a party Friday night. Couldn't see her, though. It was dark."

"I see," Julie said, raising an eyebrow. "Well, maybe *this* will help you forget that."

The rest of the world seemed miles away as they shared a long, glorious kiss, and Josh felt as though Phi Epsilon were already a distant chapter in his life.

Fifteen

Julie leaned in front of Josh and said to Elizabeth, "Jessica was fantastic!"

"The best one in the show," Josh added. "I didn't know she could be so funny!"

"I don't think she did, either!" Elizabeth answered with a broad smile.

Everyone was wildly applauding the lead players as they came out for their curtain calls. Julie could feel the tense excitement when it was time for Jessica to take her bow. Suddenly, from the wings, Jessica made a leaping, twirling entrance in a perfectly executed jeté. "Bravo!" Mr. Wakefield shouted, three seats to the right of Julie. The audience rose to its feet, and Jessica flopped onto the floor, quickly brushing herself off and giving a little curtsy.

The audience laughed approvingly, and Josh threw his fist in the air, letting out a loud yell. Julie looked past Elizabeth to see Mr. and Mrs. Wakefield practically bursting with pride.

After the last actor took his bow and the applause died away, the Wakefields, Jeffrey, Josh, and Julie all ran backstage to find Jessica. She was busy hugging and kissing the other members of the cast.

"Hey, can we tear you away for a minute, star?" Mrs. Wakefield asked. When Jessica saw her sister and her parents, she ran over and tried to throw her arms around them all.

"So, is *that* why we were paying Madame André all that money?" Mr. Wakefield joked.

"Oh, stop it, Ned," Alice Wakefield said. She turned to Jessica. "Honey, it just goes to show which side of the family you get your sense of humor from."

"Jess, you were even better than I thought you'd be," Elizabeth said. "How did you do it?"

A deep voice interrupted her. "She had the best teacher, of course!" Mr. Jaworski bellowed, coming up behind her. He went over to Jessica and gave her a hug. "And a whole lot of talent! Not very many people can play that part so well, Jessica. Congratulations."

Jessica gave her teacher a wide smile. "Well, you were so good to stick with me, even when I thought I was a pole-up-the-back, duck-walking classical ballerina—"

Suddenly Jessica stopped talking as Danielle approached. "Jessica, you were wonderful! Now I know why I didn't get this part. Nobody could have done it like you!"

"Oh, thanks, Danielle," Jessica said. "Uh, where's Bruce? Didn't he come with you?"

Danielle's smile faded. "Are you kidding? I got rid of him. I couldn't believe some of the cruel things he—" Just then she seemed to notice Julie. "Oh, well, *you* know," she said.

There was a tense silence in the room, and Julie knew that everyone was thinking about what had happened at the Phi Epsilon party. Not long ago she would have felt like crawling under the carpeting. But now . . . now she had more important things to think about. With a warm, loving glance she looked up into Josh's eyes and asked innocently, "Bruce who?"

By the time Julie, Josh, and the Wakefields finally left the school, most of the audience had already gone. As they all walked down the hallway to the front lobby, Mr. Jaworski joined them.

"Coming to the cast party, Mr. Jaworski?" Jessica asked. "We're all going to Casey's!"

"Ugh," Mr. Jaworski replied, putting a hand

on his stomach. "I made the mistake of ordering a Diet Breaker the last time I was there, and I haven't had the courage to go back since."

"I know what you mean," Josh said, and Elizabeth and Julie broke into laughter.

Jessica was the first one into the lobby, where she saw a small crowd of students gathered around Amy Sutton and Lila. They were all giggling and trying to look at something that was being passed around.

When Lila looked up to see Jessica, her face lit up. "Hey, you were *fantastic!*" she cried out.

"We were waiting for you," Amy said. "I have something to show you." She looked around the group. "OK, who's got the—"

Just then her eyes caught Mr. Jaworski coming around the corner. Quickly she reached over to Maria Santelli, grabbed something out of her hand, and hid it behind her back. Jessica tried to make out what it was, but Sally Larson and Caroline Pearce were in the way.

"Uh, hi, Mr. Jaworski," Amy said with a tight smile.

Mr. Jaworski raised an eyebrow. "Hello, Amy. Looks like you've got something pretty interesting there."

"Hmm?" Amy answered innocently. "What do you mean?"

Mr. Jaworski smiled and shook his head. "Not bad," he said. "Maybe you ought to try out for the drama club. You're a good actress."

The group around Amy giggled as Mr. Jaworski continued walking to the front door. The Wakefields were right behind him, chatting with Julie and Josh, Elizabeth and Jeffrey.

Jessica was dying to find out what was going on, but the cast party was the first thing on her mind. Right now she was just a tiny bit late—which meant it would be the perfect time to make a grand entrance.

"Come on, Jess!" Elizabeth's voice floated in from outside.

"Coming!" Jessica called, heading for the door. She glanced over her shoulder at Amy and Lila.

Amy returned her look with an impish smile. "We'll talk tomorrow," Amy said, waving goodbye. "You'll love this!"

First thing in the morning, Jessica vowed to herself as she walked out the door, *I'm going to find out what Amy is up to.*

Find out what the excitement is all about in Sweet Valley High #48, Slam Book Fever.

SWEET VALLEY HIGH®

SUPER THRILLERS

☐ **26905 DOUBLE JEOPARDY #1**   **$2.95**

When the twins get part-time jobs on the Sweet Valley newspaper, they're in for some chilling turn of events. The "scoops" Jessica invents to impress a college reporter turn into the real thing when she witnesses an actual crime—but now no one will believe her! The criminal has seen her car, and now he's going after Elizabeth. The twins have faced danger and adventure before ... but never like this!

☐ **27230 ON THE RUN #2**   **$2.95**

Elizabeth is attracted to Eric Hankman who is working with the twins at the newspaper. Eric feels the same, but he's very secretive. When the truth comes out— Eric's father testified against a mob leader and was given a new identity under a witness protection program—it leads to a deadly confrontation for Eric and Elizabeth!

Prices and availability subject to change without notice

Buy them at your local bookstore or use this page to order.

Bantam Books, Dept. SVH2, 414 East Golf Road, Des Plaines, IL 60016

Please send me the books I have checked above. I am enclosing $_____
(please add $2.00 to cover postage and handling). Send check or money order
—no cash or C.O.D.s please.

Mr/Ms _____

Address _____

City/State _____ Zip _____

SVH2—8/88

Please allow four to six weeks for delivery. This offer expires 2/89.

Special Offer
Buy a Bantam Book
for only 50¢.

Now you can order the exciting books you've been wanting to read straight from Bantam's latest catalog of hundreds of titles. *And* this special offer gives you the opportunity to purchase a Bantam book for only 50¢. Here's how:

By ordering any five books at the regular price per order, you can also choose any other single book listed (up to a $5.95 value) for only 50¢. Some restrictions do apply, so for further details send for Bantam's catalog of titles today.

Just send us your name and address and we'll send you Bantam Book's SHOP AT HOME CATALOG!